The Sweetest Waltz

De-ann Black

Text copyright © 2024 by De-ann Black
Cover Design & Illustration © 2024 by De-ann Black

All rights reserved.
No part of this book may be used or reproduced in any manner whatsoever without the written consent of the author.

This is a work of fiction. Names, characters, places, and incidents are either products of the author's imagination or are used fictitiously. Any resemblance to actual persons, living or dead, businesses, companies, events, or locales is entirely coincidental.

Paperback edition published 2024

The Sweetest Waltz

ISBN: 9798324463786

The Sweetest Waltz is the first book in the Music, Dance & Romance series.

1. The Sweetest Waltz

Also by De-ann Black (Romance, Action/Thrillers & Children's books). See her Amazon Author page or website for further details about her books, screenplays, illustrations and artwork. www.De-annBlack.com

Romance:
The Sweetest Waltz
Sweet Music
Love & Lyrics
Christmas Weddings
Fairytale Christmas on the Island
The Cure for Love at Christmas
Vintage Dress Shop on the Island
Scottish Island Fairytale Castle
Scottish Loch Summer Romance
Scottish Island Knitting Bee
Sewing & Mending Cottage
Knitting Shop by the Sea
Colouring Book Cottage
Knitting Cottage
Oops! I'm the Paparazzi, Again
The Bitch-Proof Wedding
Embroidery Cottage
The Dressmaker's Cottage
The Sewing Shop
Heather Park
The Tea Shop by the Sea
The Bookshop by the Seaside
The Sewing Bee
The Quilting Bee
Snow Bells Wedding
Snow Bells Christmas
Summer Sewing Bee
The Chocolatier's Cottage
Christmas Cake Chateau
The Beemaster's Cottage

The Sewing Bee By The Sea
The Flower Hunter's Cottage
The Christmas Knitting Bee
The Sewing Bee & Afternoon Tea
Shed In The City
The Bakery By The Seaside
The Christmas Chocolatier
The Christmas Tea Shop & Bakery
The Bitch-Proof Suit

Action/Thrillers:
Knight in Miami.
Agency Agenda.
Love Him Forever.
Someone Worse.
Electric Shadows.
The Strife of Riley.
Shadows of Murder.

Colouring books:
Summer Nature. Flower Nature. Summer Garden. Spring Garden. Autumn Garden. Sea Dream. Festive Christmas. Christmas Garden. Flower Bee. Wild Garden. Flower Hunter. Stargazer Space. Christmas Theme. Faerie Garden Spring. Scottish Garden Seasons. Bee Garden.

Embroidery books:
Floral Garden Embroidery Patterns
Floral Spring Embroidery Patterns
Christmas & Winter Embroidery Patterns
Floral Nature Embroidery Designs
Scottish Garden Embroidery Designs

Contents

Chapter One	1
Chapter Two	20
Chapter Three	33
Chapter Four	53
Chapter Five	67
Chapter Six	79
Chapter Seven	92
Chapter Eight	106
Chapter Nine	120
Chapter Ten	134
Chapter Eleven	148
Chapter Twelve	162
Chapter Thirteen	176
Chapter Fourteen	187
Chapter Fifteen	200
About De-ann Black	224

CHAPTER ONE

The small town on the east coast of Scotland near Edinburgh nestled between the glistening water of the Firth of Forth, that merged with the North Sea, and the beautiful Scottish countryside.

Sunlight streamed through the wide open door of the pretty farmhouse barn, illuminating the area where Delphie had set up her makeshift artist's studio. Easels displayed two acrylic paintings she was working on, one half finished, the other almost complete, depicting couples dancing in classic poses. The third painting, a poster–size watercolour of a couple in foxtrot mode, was taped flat to the board on her artwork table alongside a selection of watercolour paints. The overachieving, former graphic designer from the heart of Edinburgh hadn't yet slowed down to the easy rhythm of a quaint, small town life.

But that was the plan.

And she was working on it. Along with taking a chance to create a niche for herself as an independent artist, a painter, something she'd long wanted to do, but never had time for. As a graphic designer working for a company in Edinburgh, her hectic work schedule had overshadowed everything.

Attractive, thirty, her dark chestnut hair was tied back in a silky ponytail from her pale features and green eyes. Her jeans emphasised her shapely but slender figure and she hadn't yet splashed paint on her pink shirt, but the day was young. Buying an apron to protect her clothes, and tops she didn't mind getting paint splodges on, were headlining her to–do list.

In the meantime, she'd rummaged through the shirts she used to wear when she worked as a smartly–dressed designer in the city office, and chosen a pastel pink, sky blue and pale yellow to weather the paint storm.

As a bonus, this helped offload the memories of the four years in a corporate world that restricted her creativity, in more ways than one. Seeing the pristine shirts speckled with bright colours from her paintings felt uplifting. Cheerful.

Since being let go by the company when they needed to cut back on staff, and splitting up with her boyfriend when he turned out to be a cheat, there hadn't been a lot to be cheerful about.

Until recently, when her grandparents wanted her to look after their farmhouse while they went on an extended holiday to Paris to relive the romance of where they first met.

Their request coincided with Delphie wanting to get away from the city. So when her grandparents needed her help, she'd packed her bags and drove to the small town that wasn't too far from Edinburgh.

The interior of the barn had been converted years ago. It had a dance floor with an area for entertainment. A small stage, bar, a social hub. Not currently in use for anything other than Delphie's studio.

She'd laid a canvas sheet to shield the floor beneath her artwork and it extended to cover part of the dance floor. Her artwork tables and easels were set up at the side of the dance floor, near the door where the sunlight and fresh air poured in.

While she painted, an old clip from yesteryear of a couple waltzing played on her laptop. The couple, shown in their late twenties, were her grandparents. They waltzed under twinkle lights, the only two beneath the spotlight in the decorated barn. Her grandmother, a professional dancer, wore a beautiful pale pink dress. Her grandfather was suited.

Music played, a romantic ballad. The song lyrics highlighted their story...

I fell in love with you
The first time I saw you dance
That night felt like magic
Made me believe in real romance
Through the years we've been together
In love for ever
One thing is still true
I dance the sweetest waltzes with you...

The video ended and Delphie smiled to herself.

Standing back to view her watercolour painting, she went to add more cerulean blue and French ultramarine to her palette, but she was running low on both. A trip to the local art shop was in order.

But before she could pick up her bag, a video call came through on her laptop.

'Morning, Delphie,' her grandmother said, smiling at her from a hotel room in Paris. 'Painting I see. I'm so glad my old photo album is of use to you. You're such a talented artist.'

'You're biased.'

'And you're too modest. How's your artwork coming along? Selling any more paintings to the local art shop?'

'I am. I'm grateful that Callum is taking a chance on my work, and so far, he's sold several dance theme pieces I've given him to display for sale in his shop.'

Her grandmother, Delphine, was a mature, elegant woman whose Parisian heritage and professional dance background still showed in her stylish clothes. As a ballerina in her twenties, she'd performed on stage one evening in Paris and captured the heart of Billy, a young Scottish farmer on holiday in France. She'd left Paris to marry the love of her life and live in the farmhouse. They'd never been back to where they'd first fallen in love until now.

Billy's smiling face peered into frame. 'How's my favourite granddaughter?'

'She's you're only granddaughter,' his wife reminded him.

He laughed. 'Delphie would've always been my favourite. You remind me so much of...' he thumbed to his wife.

Delphine pushed him playfully. 'Hurry up and get yourself ready to go out while I talk to Delphie.'

With a smile and a wave, he was gone.

'We're heading out into the heart of Paris to a cafe that sells chocolate croissants that taste like a dream,' Delphine explained.

'Sounds delicious. I might treat myself to a chocolate cupcake from the bakery while I'm at the art shop buying more paint.'

'Is everything okay at the farmhouse? Are you settling into the slower pace of small town life?' Then her grandmother peered at the three paintings in the background and shook her head. 'Multitasking is great, but you need to ease off a little, especially when it comes to your artwork. Unless Callum wants to buy lots more paintings from you.'

'I'm trying to get out of the overachieving rut. But Callum does want more paintings from me so...' Delphie shrugged.

'A fortuitous excuse.' Her grandmother grinned knowingly. 'Callum's nice. And he's single. Maybe you could—'

'No,' Delphie cut–in. 'Romance is not on my to–do list. At least for a while. I want to settle down, find my artistic style, see if I can make this work.'

'You should always make time for romance,' her grandmother said, casting a glance towards wherever her husband had gone. 'I can't imagine how my life would've been if I hadn't taken a chance on marrying Billy and moving to the farm.' She sighed thoughtfully. 'I loved being a dancer. I really did. But I know I made the right choice to leave that life behind.'

'And now you're back after all these years, reliving where you both fell in love. What's it like?'

'Many things have changed, and yet lots are still the same, or the way that we remember them. Love tends to show everything in a rosy glow, but the theatre where I danced during the ballet, it's still there. We've bought tickets to a show. A couple of shows in fact. It's so exciting.'

'I'm happy your trip is worthwhile.'

'We're grateful to you for stepping in and looking after the farmhouse while we're jaunting around Europe.'

'It was perfect timing. I needed to get away from the city, to view my life from a whole different perspective,' said Delphie.

'An artist's perspective. Unlike your mother. The artistic gene jumped a generation. I know she's married a man who is as fascinated by finance as she is, but still...we always enjoyed when you came to stay with us at the farmhouse during the holidays.'

'I have nothing but fond memories of those times. And I'm so sorry I hadn't been back in four years. That's on me.'

'Hush now. You were busy building a career in the city. We understood. Don't beat yourself up about that.'

Delphie smiled warmly at her grandmother. Her parents hadn't approved of her giving up her life in the city when she'd told them she was moving, temporarily, to the town. But she'd held firm to wanting to go. Her life was one long list of disappointing her corporate parents while being cheered on from the sidelines by her grandparents.

Either way, here she was, trying to make a fresh start — and in need of more paint.

'I won't hold you back from your painting,' said her grandmother. 'And keep an open mind about Callum. See if there's a spark between you when you're in his art shop.'

'Okay,' Delphie conceded, while doubting it. No sparks had ignited between them so far. And from her disastrous but limited dating history those were the first things needed for the romance mix.

'Add romance to your to–do list.'

'Under needing an apron to protect my clothes from paint splashes,' Delphie joked.

'There are aprons hanging up in the kitchen cupboard. Help yourself to a couple of them.'

'I don't want to ruin your pretty aprons.'

'Nonsense. You know I love to sew. It'll give me an excuse to buy more fabric to make new aprons. And remember, if you need a dress for a special occasion, you'll find plenty in my wardrobes in the spare room. I've stored all my dance dresses there.'

Delphie went to object but her grandmother cut–in.

'Dresses are meant to be worn, not hung up and hidden for years.'

'I'll keep that in mind, though I don't anticipate needing any beautiful ball gowns or evening dresses at the moment,' said Delphie. 'But I'll take you up on your offer of the aprons.'

Her grandmother smiled. 'We're heading out now for those chocolate croissants. Have fun painting.'

'I will.'

After the call, Delphie picked up her bag and headed out into the sunshine. She breathed in the scent of the flowers and greenery from the fields. Nearby farmer friends were keeping an eye on her grandparents' property where they grew flowers, leaving Delphie free to get on with her artistic pursuits.

Getting into her car, she drove the short distance into the hub of the town.

Delphie walked briskly along the small town's main street towards the art shop clasping her voluminous but stylish bag.

The town with its quaint shops looked lovely in the morning sunlight. The fragrance from the baskets of flowers hanging from the lamp posts mingled with the fresh countryside air wafting in from the fields that surrounded the hub of the close–knit community.

It reminded her of the times when she was little and she'd stay at her grandparents' farmhouse while her parents continued their busy business lives in Edinburgh. Those holidays always felt exciting, and although she was now thirty, remained fresh in her thoughts.

She glanced at one of the paintings on display, depicting a romantic couple waltzing. The woman wore a beautiful pale pink dress and the man wore a suit. They were pictured in hold, a moment captured in the painting. The name of the painting was printed on a card: *The Sweetest Waltz*.

Without pausing, Delphie went inside the shop.

The owner, Callum, in his thirties, with brown hair and a fit build, was working on a landscape painting. His easel was set up beside the counter. He put his brush down and smiled when he saw her.

'Morning, Delphie. What can I get for you today? Or do you have any new paintings for me?'

'No new paintings, yet. I'm working on them. But I've run out of cerulean blue and French ultramarine.' She was familiar with the shop and picked up the tubes of paint she needed and put them on the counter. 'I'll stock up on a few others while I'm here.' She proceeded to select lemon yellow, magenta, raw sienna and green gold.

They chatted about art as he put the paints in a bag.

'Your new dancing couple is really catching people's interest.' He gestured to a man peering in the window at the painting. Neither of them knew the man. Wil was tall, early thirties, fit and wore smart casual clothes.

Delphie glanced at the man. He was handsome, with well–cut dark hair, but there was something else about him...

Wil didn't notice them watching him.

'And your other dance theme paintings sold well,' Callum added. He sold artwork in the shop and online. The shop's website was popular with buyers.

'Thank you for displaying my work, Callum. I really appreciate it.'

'It's a win–win for both of us.'

She noticed he was working on a landscape painting. He sold his own paintings, and those of other artists like Delphie.

'Is that a local scene?' she said, admiring his half–finished work.

'Yes, I'm trying to show the beauty of the countryside.'

'You've really captured the colours in the fields.'

Callum smiled, taking the compliment from one artist to another. Then he leaned back and viewed his painting with a critical eye.

'It could probably benefit from some figures in the scene. But as you know, I can't paint people. Not like you.'

'I can't paint landscapes like you. I've always loved painting people. Especially dancing figures.'

'You have a real talent for it.'

She smiled, paid for her paints and put them in her bag. 'Thanks again, Callum.'

As she left the shop, she glanced at the man still looking at the beautiful dancing couple painting in the window. A classic ballroom waltz pose.

Wil was so busy looking at the painting, he didn't notice her.

Delphie walked past him smiling to herself.

Wil finally went into the shop. He'd never been in before, and seeing Callum painting the landscape, assumed he was the waltzing couple artist.

'I'm interested in the painting in the window. The Sweetest Waltz.'

Callum put his brush down, wiped his hands and smiled.

'You're very talented,' said Wil. 'The way you've captured the movement of the dancers.'

'I'm not the artist. Delphie painted that one. You just missed her,' Callum told him.

Wil frowned. He hadn't noticed her. 'Is she a local artist?'

'Yes, but she's fairly new in town. I've recently started selling her work. Original paintings and limited edition prints.'

'I'm interested in the original, if it's for sale.'

'Yes, I'll let you see it.' Callum went over and lifted the painting from the window display. 'It's a beautiful painting. She's created the romance of the couple waltzing.'

Wil nodded, admiring the work. 'I'll buy it.'

'Do you want it delivered?'

'No, I'll take it with me.'

Callum started to wrap the painting.

'I'm opening a dance studio just off the main street,' said Wil.

'I heard about that. I guess the painting is for your new studio.'

'Yes, I'm trying to liven up the walls with dance artwork.' Wil glanced around. 'Do you have any other paintings or prints like this one?'

'I did, but I sold them recently. Delphie's work. Maybe you should talk to her. She's working on new paintings.' Callum rummaged in a drawer. 'Here's her card. She lives in one of the farmhouses. It belongs to her grandparents. They're on holiday in Europe, so she's looking after the property.'

Wil read the address on the card. 'This is near me.'

'If you're practically neighbours, you should take a look at her work. She's converted the barn into a temporary art studio. She only arrived recently from Edinburgh.'

'Delphie's from Edinburgh?'

'She worked as a graphic designer for a city company. Then they cut back on staff and she was let go. She said it was serendipity.'

'A happy turn of events?'

'Yes, her grandparents needed her help, and she wanted a fresh start. She says she'd always dreamed of being an artist. Painting. Making her own way.'

Wil paid for the painting and put Delphie's card in his pocket. 'I'll call her, or drop by. Thanks for your help...'

'Callum.'

'Thanks, Callum. I'm Wil.'

'Welcome to the town, Wil.'

Smiling, Wil took his painting and left.

The barn door was open wide letting the sunshine stream in. Delphie was engrossed in painting her watercolour dancing couple, a foxtrot pose. She stood back to view her work, wearing one of her grandmother's pretty floral aprons to cover her shirt and jeans.

Wil came into view, approaching from outside in the sunlight, and peered in. He halted outside the doorway, silhouetted against the farmhouse garden backdrop.

Delphie was so busy painting, she didn't notice him, at first.

'Delphie?'

She looked round and saw the man from outside the art shop now standing watching her paint.

'Yes, can I help you?'

'I bought your painting. The Sweetest Waltz.'

'I saw you looking at it in the art shop window,' she told him. Now his intense blue eyes were looking at her. The artist in her matched his eyes to the cerulean blue of her palette.

Wil tentatively stepped inside and walked towards her, with long, smooth, elegant strides, stopping at a polite distance.

'Sorry, I was so interested in the painting, I didn't notice you,' he said.

'I'll take that as a compliment.'

He cast her a warm, sexy smile, causing her to react to his good looks. Pushing the attraction aside, her artistic senses assessed him.

The angles in his handsome face were perfect for portraiture, though she sensed there were wildly different facets to his character. Which one would be the right look for this man? Strong and bold or sensual and deep?

He continued to enthuse about the painting he'd bought.

'I love how you captured the essence of the waltz. The couple's posture.'

'I worked from an old photograph.' She gestured to a table where the photo album sat alongside her art portfolio. 'And an old video. I wanted the couple's stance and hold to be right.'

'You've nailed it. I'm Wil, by the way. I'm opening a new dance studio in town.'

'How exciting.' She smiled. 'I thought I recognised you. I saw you perform in Edinburgh. You're an incredible dancer.'

'That's very kind of you to say.'

'So you're starting up a dance studio. Are you from the town?'

'No, Edinburgh, the same as you.'

She frowned.

'Callum told me,' he explained. 'He gave me your card. I'm interested in other paintings for my studio.'

She focussed on the one she was working on.

Wil came over for a closer look.

'It's not a waltz, it's a—'

'Foxtrot,' Wil cut–in.

'Right.' She went over to the other table and showed him her art portfolio. It contained predominantly dance and figurative work. 'These are recent paintings that Callum sold as limited edition prints and originals.'

'They're gorgeous. I notice you use different techniques, though I'm no expert on art.'

'I work in various mediums. Oils, acrylics, watercolours and pen and ink.'

'The city company's loss.'

She frowned again.

'Callum told me about your previous job as a graphic designer.'

'Ah, Callum has been chatty.'

'I pried. He said you'd always dreamed of being an artist.'

'Some dreams do come true.' She went back over to her watercolour painting.

'You have a true talent for painting dancers.'

'I enjoy painting people, and dancing seems so romantic. I love the movement of the figures. The flow of the dresses. The posture and the sense of the music.'

'So, you're a romantic,' he said.

'Only when it comes to my art.'

'Not personally?'

'I used to be. But now it's easier to paint romance than risk another broken heart.' She quickly changed the subject back to her artwork. 'Is there anything you like? Any particular style of painting?'

'I'm not sure exactly what I need for my studio. Certainly The Sweetest Waltz.'

'I could take a look at your studio and give you some suggestions,' she offered.

'That would be great. It's just off the main street. The old community hall. I've leased it for a year.'

'I'll drop by this afternoon, unless you're teaching classes.'

'I'm not teaching dance classes. The studio is for my personal use, and to work with professional dancers on their choreography for stage performances and competitions.'

'Have you given up performing or competing?'

'I'm stepping aside for a little while.' He kept his reply vague. The gossip about his last dance partner, Sienna, leaving him to compete with someone else had recently hit the gossip columns. But he hoped to fit into the small town community, while keeping to the background.

His name still cropped up in dance news, especially as this was the second dance partner he'd parted ways with in the past few years. Not by choice. He hadn't anticipated they'd ditch him for other dancers. Perhaps his training was too intense? No, he told himself. It was because of love. They'd wanted to be his girlfriends and he had dated the former before they separated when she found someone else to compete with.

Then Sienna left him days before a large contest to dance with his closest rival. That one had stung, though he kept the sting to himself and moved away from Edinburgh to relax and recoup in the small town. It wasn't too far away from the city, but far enough to be a discouraging distance for those thinking of dropping by his new studio to see what he was doing.

Scouring suitable locations, he'd found the small town on a map. He'd driven there, and taking a look around, he liked the feeling of the community instantly.

Checking the local paper for a hall or venue to lease, he'd seen that the old hall off main street was available. A new community hall had replaced it.

Wil was wealthy, from his family's background, and his success as a dance performer and competitor. He'd recently started to work as a choreographer too, and when he had a look at the hall, he'd made a snap decision and taken it for one year. A year out to gauge what direction he wanted to take his career. Dance would be at the heart of it. Nothing would change that. His love of dance hadn't waned even when he'd had his heart ripped out by being ditched by his dance partners.

Brushing aside these thoughts, he studied the old photos in the album of a couple dancing. He noticed the template for The Sweetest Waltz.

'That's my grandparents,' said Delphie. 'My grandmother was a professional dancer. She taught my grandfather to waltz.'

'Callum says you're taking care of the farm while they're on holiday.'

'They're in Paris. Reliving where they first met.'

Wil seemed interested to hear what had happened.

'My grandmother was performing on stage in a show. My grandfather said he fell in love with her seeing her dance.'

'Now that is romantic.'

'They met after the performance and...she moved here. They got married and lived happily ever after.'

Wil read the name Delphine on one of the photos. '*Delphine?*'

'My grandmother is from Paris. I'm named after her.'

'Did your grandmother continue dancing when she moved here?'

'Not professionally, just for the love of dance.'

Wil noticed the dance floor. He tapped and tested it. 'I see the barn has a dance floor.'

'My grandparents had it converted years ago so they could dance. Then they used it for local party events. Dance nights at weekends are popular.'

'Did you ever go?'

'Once or twice. But I hadn't visited here in four years. I was too busy with work in the city. I should've made time.'

Wil found a space on the floor and danced a little. 'This is a nice floor.' He gazed around him. 'I can picture it all lit up. The music, the atmosphere. You should hold dance nights here again.'

'I think I'll concentrate on my art.'

'Sorry, I have a tendency to be bossy.'

'I do too.'

'Then come along to my dance studio this afternoon and tell me what artwork I need to brighten it up.'

'I will.'

Smiling, he walked out of the barn. 'I live nearby. I'm leasing the house just down the road, the one with the lovely flower garden.'

Delphie nodded acknowledgement, and then watched him drive away.

Wil drove along the country road, with a glance at his house as he went by. The property was traditional with a surrounding garden, and had only recently become his residence. So different from his flat in Edinburgh.

Wil pulled up outside the old community hall just off the main street. No sign at the front entrance that it was his dance studio. He'd hired local people to help him transform it.

Lifting the painting from the back of his car, he carried it inside.

The entrance comprised of a small reception area with a desk. The decor was sleek and stylish with few unnecessary embellishments, and led through to the main part of the dance studio where there was a dance floor that Wil found to be excellent.

The walls were painted cream, with sophisticated lighting illuminating the studio. Large mirrors on one wall reflected the lights and doubled the size of the studio that was already spacious. A barre for stretching and warming up was erected in front of the mirrors and could be lifted aside when necessary. The dance floor had been the selling point as far as Wil was concerned. Well sprung. Not too firm. Not too soft. Ideal for dancing.

Now all Wil wanted was to spruce up the decor with some dance theme artwork.

Standing in the middle of the dance floor, he viewed the empty walls, wondering where to hang his new painting. Deciding that he wanted it to be seen prominently, he hung it on one of the main walls.

Looking around, he wondered what artwork Delphie would advise when she dropped by in the afternoon. For some reason, he couldn't get her out of his thoughts. She was certainly beautiful and talented. Shaking away such thoughts, he decided to put on some classic music and dance on his own, spinning around the room, feeling the energy that always ignited in him when he was dancing.

CHAPTER TWO

Delphie finished painting the foxtrot watercolour. She smiled as she studied the final look of it, the way the vibrancy of the colours enhanced the flow of the couple's pose and captured the movement of the dress.

Depending on the type of dance and pose, drawn from the old photos in the album, Delphie created each painting using a variety of mediums. The foxtrot suited the watercolour effect. It had a dreamlike quality to it.

Steeped in her artwork, she suddenly blinked and checked the time. She had to get changed out of her painting clothes and into something more suitable to visit Wil's new dance studio.

Taking a quick photograph of the foxtrot painting that was still taped flat to the board to dry thoroughly, she grabbed her portfolio and her bag, and then hurried over to the farmhouse to get ready.

The traditional farmhouse had changed little over the years and still retained the homely feeling that Delphie loved. She remembered being excited to visit during the holidays. Often her parents stayed to work in Edinburgh and her grandparents would drive to the city to pick her up. She especially loved the farmhouse at Christmastime when she'd help to decorate the tree outside the front door with sparkling ornaments and lights.

She learned to bake cakes in the farmhouse kitchen, and loved to ice them and add sprinkles. Her grandparents were a happy couple, and she hoped one day to have a relationship like that. So far, all she'd had were broken promises and broken hearts.

The kitchen was the hub of the farmhouse, and no matter what time of year it was, it felt comforting and welcoming. Her grandmother's sewing machine often whirred in the background as she stitched quilts, table covers and cushions to match the decor. Delphie had learned how to sew and knit. She particularly enjoyed knitting woolly hats and scarves. Though she hadn't knitted anything in years due to her busy schedule, she'd had a notion to pick up a pair of knitting needles and a ball of double knit yarn from her grandmother's stash.

The spacious farmhouse had other rooms that Delphie could've used to set up her art studio, but she loved the idea of using the barn.

And she thought about Wil, standing there in the barn admiring her artwork.

Pushing such thoughts aside, Delphie dashed upstairs to the spare bedroom where she was staying while her grandparents were away. It was comfy, and one of her grandmother's handmade quilts adorned the bed. The window had a view of the surrounding countryside and fields.

On the wall was a painting she'd done years ago, a landscape depicting the farmhouse and the countryside. Unlike Callum's landscape, it included people, little figures busy in the fields. An early work, it wasn't one of her best, but it was one of her most loved, especially as she'd attempted to paint her grandparents standing together at the front of the farmhouse.

Rummaging through her wardrobe, she lifted out a fashionable dress that she used to wear in the city and put it on. Letting her hair down from the ponytail, she brushed it smooth, stepped into a pair of heels, refreshed her lipstick and then hurried out to her car.

On the drive down to the dance studio, she glanced at Wil's house with the lovely garden. Continuing on, she found herself looking forward to having a peek around the new studio, and to seeing Wil again. Reminding herself that romance wasn't on her to–do list, she swept the fit, handsome image of Wil from her thoughts and wondered what type of paintings would enhance his studio.

The drive was a short one, eventually taking her past the bakery shop as she pulled up outside the old community hall. An eclectic mix of shops were situated along the street, many with pretty canopies.

Stepping out of the car, armed with her portfolio and a mind full of ideas, she noted that there was nothing on the exterior of the entrance to indicate that a new dance studio was inside. But she reckoned that if Wil had no intention of teaching regular dance classes, it was smart not to advertise it.

She admired the stylish decor of the reception area, and wondered if he wanted any paintings for the walls, or perhaps it was only for the main part of the dance studio. The reception was more of a token gesture rather than a working requirement. Sparse, sleek.

Music filtered out from the heart of the studio and she followed the sound and peeked in.

Wil was in full dance mode, as if he was performing a stage number. The music was upbeat.

'Hi,' she said, but her voice was drowned out by the music.

She stood there for a moment, entranced by his strength, artistry and skill.

'Wil!' Delphie finally called out to him.

He stopped and spun around at the sound of his name.

For a second, seeing the beautiful young woman in a lovely dress standing there in his studio, he was taken aback. Of course he recognised her, but with her silky chestnut hair worn down, and the jeans and shirt replaced with a dress and heels, she'd caught him delightfully off guard.

'Oh, sorry.' He ran over to the music system and switched it off. He wore dark trousers and a white shirt, open at the neck. He'd changed to look extra smart for her arrival, but then ended up dancing while waiting for her.

He suppressed the urge to keep the music playing and take Delphie in hold and waltz with her around the floor. But a non dancer like her might find it daunting being invited to waltz the moment she'd stepped into the studio.

'Was that a piece from a stage performance?' she said.

Wil swept his hair back from his forehead and walked towards her with long, fluid strides. 'No, it's a new dance routine I've been choreographing.'

'It's impressive.' He was impressive too, but she kept that remark to herself.

He gestured around him. 'First impressions, what do you think?'

'The studio is lovely. I can see that the walls have been freshly painted, but they are a little bit bare.'

'I had them painted cream to lighten the room up, and added mirrors and extra lighting,' he explained.

Delphie walked to the middle of the dance floor. 'I like the atmosphere of your studio. There's an uplifting energy to it. Though perhaps it's all the energy you've whipped up from your dancing,' she added with a smile.

Wil smiled back at her. 'When I first viewed the premises, I liked the atmosphere. As you say, there's an uplifting energy to it. I thought that it would be perfect for dancing.' He tapped the floor with his dance shoes. 'And the floor is excellent.'

Delphie saw her reflection in the mirrors, and blinked, seeing herself for the first time standing with Wil nearby. Captured in the background of the image was her Sweetest Waltz painting. Something jolted inside her, and she turned away from the mirrors and showed him her portfolio.

'I've added some sketches of dance figures that I intend painting,' she said.

Wil looked with interest at her work. 'Is this how your paintings start?'

'Yes, everything starts with a pencil drawing, then I use that as the template for a painting.'

He took charge of the portfolio and turned the pages to see the extent of her range. 'Some of these sketches are pieces of art in themselves.' He stopped at a sketch that had been inked.

'I draw in pen and ink as well as paint watercolours, oils and acrylics,' she explained.

'These three pen and ink drawings would make a lovely set for the reception wall.'

The idea hadn't occurred to her, but she tilted her head and viewed them with a fresh eye. 'Yes, you're right.'

'Can I have these?' He corrected himself. 'What I mean is, can I buy them?'

'Of course, but they'd obviously need to be framed.'

'Callum at the art shop would do that surely.'

'He would. Warm white or beige frames would suit the pen and ink, and work well with your cream wall decor.'

Wil nodded firmly, liking her idea. He took a deep breath and glanced around. 'Okay, that's the reception taken care of. What's missing in here that would add a dash of colour and class to the walls?'

'I see you've hung up The Sweetest Waltz. I like where you've put it.' She thought for a moment and then showed him the photo of the watercolour painting on her phone. 'I finished painting the foxtrot. The colours are quite vibrant.'

Wil's face lit up. 'I love the colours and the watercolour effect is gorgeous. I'll buy that one too and have Callum frame it.'

'It'll need a border to finish the look of it,' she advised. 'But light beige would suit it.'

'Would you be able to come with me to the art shop to help select the proper borders and frames?'

Delphie smiled and nodded. 'The watercolour is still in the barn, but I'll drop it off at the art shop at a time that suits us both.'

'Right, what else?' said Wil, sounding enthusiastic. 'Do you have any other ideas? There's plenty of space on the walls.'

The designer in her had an idea. 'Apart from artwork, you could add twinkle lights to that wall over there. Drape them like I've seen in stage backgrounds to create a theatrical effect.'

'A wall of twinkle lights, yes, that would work. I plan to choreograph dance routines for professional couples and work with some of them online. I've set up cameras so I can instruct them, and I'll invite others to the studio to rehearse. But I still want a few more paintings.'

Delphie referenced her portfolio again. 'These sketches are rough, but as you can see, they portray various couples dancing.'

Wil leaned close, and she was aware of how tall he was in comparison to her. She barely came up to his broad shoulders.

'A quickstep,' he said, correctly naming the first dance pose.

'Yes, and this is obviously a tango.' She turned the pages of the portfolio. 'And this is a scene from one of my grandmother's dances. A dramatic stage performance.'

'It's a classic. And is this your grandmother as a ballerina?'

'Yes. I paint mainly couples dancing, but I want to include a single ballerina,' she said.

'I like that each painting highlights a specific style of dance. This would be perfect for the studio. Can I commission you to paint these for me?'

'I'll paint them, and if you like them, then you can buy them, or buy one or two,' she suggested.

'If you're sure.'

'I am. It'll allow me to paint freely, without pressure. I'm trying to get away from that type of lifestyle. Though you wouldn't guess from seeing several paintings I'm currently working on.'

Wil's blue eyes gazed at her as if he understood. 'It's taking me time to slow down from the fast pace that I was living.' He shrugged. 'I couldn't even wait until you arrived. I had to dance.'

'We both need time to adjust. Though knowing my nature, I'll have learned to slow down only when it's time for me to leave and go back to my busy life in the city.'

'That's my problem too. I've given myself a year to rethink what I want to do in the world of dance.'

'I've heard that competitive dancers sometimes take time out to rest and recoup. Not that I'm suggesting you're burned out or anything like that.'

'I'm not, thankfully. Not physically anyway. Perhaps a little frazzled personally.' His words trailed off.

'I don't know everything about your current situation. But I did take a sneak peek at you online after you left the barn and saw—'

'The gossip about me breaking up with two of my dance partners?'

Delphie pressed her lips together and nodded.

'Sienna was my last dance partner. We were never romantically involved, and that was the problem, on her part.'

Delphie spoke up. 'I saw you dance with Sienna in Edinburgh. You were performing in a show.'

He felt slightly relieved that she understood his recent break up with Sienna. 'We danced well together.'

'You did.' Delphie's response was half–hearted.

'Sienna is an excellent dancer,' he conceded. 'What did you think of her performance?'

Delphie hesitated.

'From an audience member's perspective,' he added, encouraging her to tell him.

Tell him the truth, she urged herself. 'I was too busy watching you dance to fully appreciate her ability. I did think the whole performance, as a couple, was wonderful.' But it was Wil who'd captured her attention that night in the theatre, not Sienna.

'People have said that we were well–matched, but my retired dance instructor always thought there was an emotional disconnection between us. He came to watch our stage performances and when we took part in competitions. He said we were certainly good together, but never magnificent.'

Delphie found herself nodding, agreeing with his dance instructor.

'Sienna left shortly before we were due to compete in a championship event,' he said. 'She'd found a new partner, my closest rival. I had no time to find a replacement, and I think I probably lost heart. A bit of both,' he concluded.

'I've split up with him,' Sienna announced, strutting into the dance studio looking like a fashion model in a designer dress and heels.

Like a tidal wave of emotional discord, Sienna swept into Wil's world again, causing a riptide of unwanted memories to flood back.

Sienna was thirty, taller than Delphie, with burnished auburn hair and pale blue eyes that iced the artist to the core.

Delphie glanced at Wil for an explanation, unsure whether Sienna was expected or still part of his life despite what he'd just told her.

Dismissing Delphie, Sienna made a beeline for Wil.

'Sienna! What are you doing here?' he said, glaring at her.

'I heard you'd opened a new dance studio.' Sienna closed in on him, but he stepped back. 'I wanted to see what you were up to.'

If Delphie hadn't been there, Wil wasn't sure what his reply would've been. But thrown by her unexpected arrival, his senses were cast to the wind.

'Rehearsing a new routine,' Wil told Sienna boldly, and so assured that even Delphie believed him until he added... 'With my new dance partner.'

Cold blue eyes iced Delphie. Clearly the last thing Sienna expected was that she'd been cheerfully replaced.

Without hesitation, Wil introduced them, hoping Delphie would go along with the ruse, at least until Sienna had left. 'Sienna, this is Del—'

'Delphine,' Delphie cut–in, giving her full name. It seemed apt to go for the total impact.

Sienna's eyes showed that the name hit the bullseye.

Wil took a deep breath, knowing that Delphie was prepared to go along with his plan.

'Delphine is my new dance partner,' Wil reiterated with a smile.

The ruse looked like it was in danger of being exposed as Sienna's eyes raked her apparent new rival from head to toe and then shook her head. 'No, I don't think she's a dancer. She wouldn't know a plié from a pirouette.'

For the first time, Sienna spoke to Delphie. 'No offence intended.'

Delphie's city savvy kicked into high gear. 'Offence taken.' There was a challenging note to her tone.

Sensing that a standoff was in danger of escalating, Wil swept Sienna aside. 'Let's talk privately in reception.' Then he said to Delphie, 'I'll be back in a few minutes.'

Delphie smiled brightly. 'That's fine, Wil. I'll just practise a plié.' Without faltering for a second, Delphie performed a perfect dancer's plié. 'And my pirouettes.' Then she spun around like a highly trained ballerina, spinning at speed several times before stopping near the mirrors.

The look of surprise on Wil's face outshone the jealous glare Sienna was sending her.

Turning on her heels, Sienna let herself be swept away by Wil.

Before disappearing into the reception, Wil looked back at Delphie, opened his arms wide and stared at Delphie in sheer amazement.

Delphie smiled sweetly and shrugged.

Wil disappeared into reception with his former partner. His mind was spinning as fast as Delphie's pirouettes. Delphie could dance! He hadn't considered this, taken only by her talent as an artist. No wonder her paintings portrayed the dance figures so well. Not only was she using the old photographs, she was able to add authenticity to the poses from her own experience. He was so steeped in surprise that Sienna's shrill words washed over him.

'Are you even listening to me?' Sienna snapped at him.

Clearly he wasn't. 'You shouldn't have come here.'

'I wanted to surprise you.' She softened her tone. 'I thought that we should talk. There's a competition due. We planned to enter before we broke up.'

'I'm not interested in competing with you.'

Sienna smiled at him. 'I think we could win, if we started rehearsing now. If you're working on a new routine, we could perform that. Your choreography was always great.'

'No, I have a new dance partner.'

She stepped close. 'I don't think that Delphine is quite your type.'

Wil stepped back. 'I believe she's my perfect match.'

'If you're still mad at me for partnering with someone else—'

'I'm not.'

'He was a mistake,' she said. 'But I'm back now. This competition is perfect for us. And now that you have your own private dance studio, we could rehearse here.'

Wil shook his head. 'No. What we had is over.' Wil knew the competition she was referring to. He kept up to date with everything that was going on in the dance world. But his plans didn't include competing again, at the moment.

Sienna remained confident. 'I'm staying in the town's main hotel for a few days. When you reconsider, you'll find me there. Or call me. We were always excellent when we danced together.'

'But never magnificent,' he added.

Forcing a smile while seething, Sienna strutted away, leaving Wil in no doubt that she still wanted to partner with him.

CHAPTER THREE

Unable to resist having a whole dance floor to herself, Delphie spun and waltzed on her own around the room under the lights, remembering how much she used to love dancing.

Wil came in, smiled, and in a fluid movement stepped close and danced with her around the floor.

Momentarily taken aback, Delphie then let Wil lead her in a waltz. Her heart soared as they danced a traditional waltz, before Wil added a few flourishes that Delphie kept in step with, and they ended close together in hold.

Delphie gazed up at Wil, slightly breathless from excitement rather than exertion. And in that moment, she sensed a spark between them.

Wil felt it too, and stepped back, smiling politely.

'I couldn't resist trying out your dance floor,' she told him, feeling a blush form across her cheeks.

He playfully listed off her accomplishments. 'Artist, dancer...any other hidden talents I should know about?'

'Troublemaker,' she admitted jokingly.

'Duly noted.'

'Though I don't think I'm the main culprit today,' she added.

'I assume you heard my conversation with Sienna.'

'I didn't want to turn the music on in case I messed with your sound system,' she explained. 'So I couldn't help but overhear the gist of it.'

Wil looked serious. 'I apologise for involving you in the predicament. I don't know why I said that you were my new dance partner. I didn't expect her to turn up like that. But thanks for going along with it.'

'I heard Sienna mention the dance competition,' she remarked. 'Are you sure you don't want to compete, especially as she seemed certain that the two of you could win.'

'I don't want to compete again with Sienna,' he said firmly. 'That chapter of my life is over.'

'If she's staying in town, she seems to think you'll change your mind.'

'I won't.' He sounded adamant.

'What about the new dance routine you were working on? Was that for the competition?'

'It was an idea I had for choreography. A few dancers have expressed an interest in having me teach them new routines.' He glanced around. 'I'm not officially open yet, though I sort of am as I'm expecting one or two professional dance couples to contact me this week with a view to learning routines for the competitive circuit.'

'Perhaps you should've explained that to Sienna,' she suggested.

'Maybe, but I wasn't anticipating her turning up out of the blue like that. It threw me. That's why I said we were a couple.' He quickly clarified. 'A dance couple.'

Delphie turned the focus back to her art portfolio.

'I'll push on with some of the paintings.'

She went to leave, but Wil spoke up.

'Where did you learn to dance like that? I don't remember seeing you on the competitive circuits.'

'My grandmother taught me when I was a wee girl, and I took dance lessons in Edinburgh,' she explained. 'I never wanted to compete. I wanted to perform on stage in shows.'

'Why didn't you?'

His phone rang, interrupting them.

'It's a long story for another time,' she said. 'I'll see myself out.'

She left him to take the call.

Outside the dance studio, she put the portfolio in her car, then walked along to the nearby bakery shop.

A pretty canopy shielded the front window from the sunlight. The aroma of vanilla, chocolate and gingerbread wafted in the air as Delphie went inside.

The owners, Catriona and Kian, a happy couple in their forties, tended to their customers. Several tables were occupied by people enjoying tea, cake and snacks.

Catriona smiled. 'Hello, Delphie, what can I get for you?'

Delphie eyed the delicious selection of cakes and savoury treats on display in the front counter.

'A chocolate cupcake please, Catriona. Unless you have a chocolate croissant.'

Kian spoke up after serving tea to customers at a table. 'We used to have chocolate croissants on the menu. I should add them again.'

'My grandmother is in Paris, and she was telling me about the croissants,' Delphie explained.

'Come back tomorrow,' said Kian. 'I'll bake some and add them to our menu.'

Delphie smiled. 'I don't want you to go to any trouble for me, Kian.'

'No trouble, Delphie. Besides, customers used to love them.'

Catriona bagged a chocolate cupcake for Delphie. She paid and then left the shop.

The street was cast in an amber glow of fading sunlight as the day unwound. The fresh scent of the sea wafted up from the shore, mingling with the country air.

Delphie felt as if nature was encouraging her to unwind too, but she had other plans.

That night, after dinner, Delphie was in the barn, working on the paintings, sketching, making a start on two canvases and a couple of watercolours. The overachiever was in full production mode.

Twinkle lights illuminated the barn, along with the lamps that highlighted her work area.

She'd used her sketches and drawn them on to the canvases and the heavy quality watercolour paper as light pencil outlines.

Opting for acrylic paint for the canvases rather than oil paint, she painted the dancing figures, referencing the photos in the album for the fluid lines of the dresses and exact posture for the poses.

The backgrounds were unfussy so that the figures were the focus. She'd painted the backgrounds first in light neutral tones, so she could then concentrate on the figures. The two backgrounds were similar in tone so that they would complement each other.

Bold reds and vibrant hues brought the tango artwork to life, but she intended to work on it over a few days, building up the structure, working from dark to light values.

Although the watercolours were drawn, she decided to leave the actual painting until the morning. The technique to create beautiful transparency required her full concentration. And for the watercolours, she aimed to work from light to dark colours.

The whole process was exciting, and she enjoyed painting with a purpose. Certainly, she'd been painting recently with the intention of selling her work via the local art shop and her website. But it felt encouraging to paint these for Wil's dance studio, and she was inspired to push ahead with the paintings.

The night air was calm with barely a breeze wafting in through the wide open barn door, and as it turned to midnight, she told herself to be sensible and put her brushes down until the morning.

It was only when she'd finished cleaning up that she noticed a message on her phone from Wil.

Are you free to come with me to the art shop tomorrow morning, around eleven?

Delphie typed her reply.

I am. See you then. And I've made a start on your paintings this evening.

She didn't expect to receive an instant reply.

I can't wait to see them. Goodnight, Cinderella.
Very funny, Wil.

Putting her phone in the pocket of her jeans, she switched off the lamps in the barn and walked over to the farmhouse. A light shone from the kitchen, warm and reassuring.

Before going inside, she gazed up at the vast night sky sprinkled with hundreds of stars. She loved the clear skies here. It made her feel like she was standing in a real life painting. A content little figure outside the farmhouse.

Breathing in the night air, she headed inside and got ready for bed.

Delphie parked her car near the bakery shop the next morning and walked along carrying her bag and portfolio containing the foxtrot watercolour painting. As she headed to the main street, Wil came running out of the dance studio.

'Delphie!'

She paused and waited for him and they walked along towards the art shop together.

Wearing a denim jacket over a floral dress, her look was a blend of fashionable casual. His smart casual clothes quietly indicated money and class.

'I've got the foxtrot painting and the pen and ink drawings,' she said. 'I phoned Callum to tell him we were coming in for frames and borders.'

'Great. Thanks for making time to do this.'

She was aware of how tall he was as they kept in step with each other. 'I was planning to drop by the bakery. Kian promised to bake chocolate croissants for me.' She explained what had happened.

'They sound delicious. I might be tempted to try one. I keep meaning to go into the bakery shop, but haven't done it yet.'

'You're lucky that it's so near your studio. They have a great lunch menu. I can recommend it.'

'I'll give it a go,' he said.

By now they'd reached the art shop. One of Callum's seascapes filled the gap where Delphie's painting had been in the front window. It depicted the local shore. The beach was picturesque, with clean golden sand, and stretched far along the coast with wonderful views over the glistening sea. A short walk from the main street, Delphie reminded herself that she wanted to make the most of it while she was in town.

'Is that the local shore?' said Wil, noticing the painting.

'It is. I used to love spending the day down the shore with my grandparents when I visited during the school summer holidays. I know that memories are often wrapped in a rosy glow, but it really is gorgeous. You should make time to have a meander down there.'

'I enjoy swimming, so I'll do that. The summer is lingering well even as we're approaching autumn,' he remarked.

They went inside the art shop.

Callum smiled, expecting them, and had put a selection of border samples and frames on the counter ready for them.

Delphie opened her portfolio and carefully handed Callum the watercolour. 'We were thinking of light beige for the border and frame.'

Callum showed them a few samples. 'This range of neutrals would work well.'

Delphie held some of the borders up beside the painting. 'What do you think, Wil?'

'I like this one.'

'It complements the tones,' said Delphie. 'This frame would look lovely with it.'

Wil nodded.

Callum noted the colours and then they moved on to selecting frames for the three pen and ink pieces.

'I like the light cream frames,' said Wil.

Happy with their choices, they left the artwork with Callum, to be collected by Wil when the paintings were ready.

Stepping out into the sunlight, they walked back round to the side street together, chatting about painting.

'Do you paint?' Delphie said to Wil.

'Nooo, but I'd love to try.'

'You should. Can you draw?'

'I was never any good at art, but I liked dabbling with paint when I was at school. I like the idea of messing around with the colours.'

'Drop by the barn sometime and try your hand at painting,' she offered.

'I don't want to interrupt your work.'

'I'm used to working in the graphic design office where there was constant creative chaos. Trust me, I can work even when there's a thunderstorm.'

'Okay, it's a date.' He instantly rephrased. 'Not a date, date. An invitation to cause chaos in the barn while you create masterpieces.'

Delphie laughed. 'That could be fun.'

She stopped and put her portfolio in her car, thinking that Wil would head into his dance studio, but instead he lingered.

'Can I tempt you with something?' said Wil.

She glanced up at him and frowned.

'Lunch at the bakery shop?' he offered. 'My treat.'

Delphie smiled and nodded. 'Yes, but be warned. Their lunches are so tasty. You could be tempted to drop by on a regular basis.'

Wil laughed and escorted her along to the bakery shop. The door was open as they approached.

'It smells delicious from here,' he said.

'Wait until you try their daily specials.'

They went in and sat down at a table near the window.

Catriona approached ready to take their order. 'Sitting in today, Delphie?'

'Yes, and this is Wil. He owns the dance studio. He's spoiling me today,' said Delphie.

'Your boyfriend should spoil you,' Catriona said chirpily.

'Oh, no, we're not...' Delphie pointed between them. 'We're just working together.'

Catriona smiled and shrugged. 'But you look like such a cute couple.'

Wil tried not to laugh at Delphie blushing.

Kian waved over to Delphie and pointed at the cake display. 'Chocolate croissants. As promised. And hello, Wil. Welcome to the town.'

'Thank you,' Wil said, smiling over at him.

Catriona proceeded to take their order of the day's special roast vegetable and cheese bake with a crisp green salad. Kian put two of the croissants aside for them.

As they enjoyed lunch, Wil smiled at Delphie. 'Tell me that long story now about your dancing.'

'Well, as I said, my grandmother first taught me, and I took dance lessons in Edinburgh. I studied ballet, ballroom, Latin American dance and modern stage.'

'But you never wanted to compete?' He prompted her to explain.

'No, I loved dancing and wanted to perform in shows on stage rather than compete in dance contests.'

'Why then did you give up dancing?'

'Real life got in the way of my dancing dreams. My parents always wanted me to work in finance with them, but that was never my thing. I loved art and dancing. When it came to selecting a career path, I was going to dance auditions for shows, but was never lucky enough to be picked. One week I attended two auditions for stage shows, and an interview for the graphic design job.' She sighed heavily. 'I was turned down for the dancing, but offered the design job. I took the job.'

'A sensible decision. But surely you could've continued with your dancing,' he reasoned.

'I thought that in my spare time I could dance. And that I could paint.' She shook her head. 'But the job very quickly took up all my spare time. There was no time for anything else. I didn't even visit my grandparents for four years.'

'What happened next?'

Wil ate his lunch and listened as she continued.

'The week I lost my job, my boyfriend split up with me. We'd been dating for two years.'

'I'm sorry. That must've been harsh.'

'It was rough, especially as I didn't see any of those pitfalls coming for me.' She shrugged. 'But he turned out to be untrustworthy. So when my grandparents wanted me to look after their farmhouse, I jumped at the chance to get away from Edinburgh, away from everything. To try a fresh start with my painting.'

'What about dancing?'

'My schedule is already full with the art. And I'm trying to slow down the pace.'

'I feel bad about giving you all this artwork to do for me.'

'No, that's fine. I want to paint. I wish I'd made more time for the things I love. Now I have a chance to see if I can succeed as an artist.'

'How long are you staying in the town?'

'Until my grandparents come home to the farmhouse. A few months. They're really enjoying their long holiday. And I love it here, so I'm in no hurry to head back to Edinburgh.'

'Any chance that you could stay? Move to the town?'

'I'm in the same predicament as you. My career will probably take me back to the city, as will yours.'

'We could meet up for lunch in Edinburgh.' He tried to sound chirpy.

'People easily forget each other in the city.' She ate her lunch, feeling a twinge of sadness in this.

'I'd never forget you, Delphie.'

She glanced at him and saw his gorgeous blue eyes gazing at her.

They both blinked out of the moment and chatted about the food.

'The bakery is going to be my regular lunch venue,' said Wil.

Kian served up their chocolate croissants and tea. 'Glad to hear it.'

Smiling, Delphie and Wil talked about art and dancing while indulging in the rich chocolate croissants.

After lunch, Wil walked Delphie back to her car.

'Thanks for lunch,' she said.

'Any time.'

'I'll keep you updated on your paintings.'

Wil nodded, walked on towards his dance studio, and glanced back seeing her get into her car and drive off.

The barn was aglow in the night as Delphie happily worked on the paintings. She'd painted the background of one of the watercolours and was now painting the figures.

Despite finding painting relaxing, she felt excitement bubbling up inside her every time Wil crossed her mind. Which was often. Too often. Sitting having lunch with him in the bakery shop was foremost in her thoughts. The way he'd looked at her when he said he'd never forget her was forged into her memory.

Shaking herself back into full concentration, she continued to paint, using soft shades of blue for the woman's dress, based on her grandmother's ball gown. The photo album was filled with images of beautiful dresses from the past.

Forcing herself to finish up well before midnight, she tidied her paints away, and before switching the lights off in the barn, she glanced back. There was the dance floor, partly covered with the drop sheet.

For a moment she pictured the barn alight with music and dancing, people enjoying themselves at a party night.

Walking over to the floor, she stood in the middle, highlighted by the twinkle lights. Wearing comfy pumps with her jeans and shirt, she did an impromptu pirouette, stopping before she reached the area protected by the sheeting.

Pulling the sheet aside at the edge of the floor to reveal the full area, she danced, gently at first, as if her comfy flat shoes were ballet pumps, gracefully performing a ballet routine from her past.

The classic music played in her head, and she finished with a flourish, extending one arm up as if pointing to the stars.

Realising she'd become distracted from that early night she'd promised herself, she turned the lights off and headed out of the barn to the farmhouse.

Another night sky filled with stars arched above her. Glancing up, she continued on into the farmhouse, planning to get a cosy night's sleep.

Wil's energy levels had soared for the rest of the day since he'd had lunch with Delphie. He admitted to himself that he liked her. But there was no room for romance in either of their lives, especially as heartbreak loomed strong. Their current situations were temporary, and he wasn't interested in a fleeting romance, despite what the gossip said about him.

He'd found a shop in the town that sold twinkle lights and spent the afternoon hanging them up, creating that wall of sparkling stage–like illumination that Delphie had suggested.

The glistening wall was an ideal backdrop for his video choreography instruction, and he'd already spoken to a couple of professional dancers about helping them with new routines.

In the evening, Wil was working on a routine when a video call came through from Gareth, someone he knew from Edinburgh. Gareth was responsible for auditioning dancers for suitable roles for stage performances, and to match couples up for contests.

'Your new studio looks enticing,' said Gareth, having heard about Wil's new studio. Similar in age to Wil, Gareth was a good looking man, fit and strong, with light brown hair and grey eyes that viewed the studio with interest.

'I'm having an open evening soon,' Wil told him, holding up the phone to let Gareth have a look around. 'I've invited other dancers to attend. You're welcome to come along to the studio.'

'I'll do that. Is it okay if I bring a couple of dancers that I hope you'll consider creating a routine for?

They're planning to compete soon, but their routine isn't quite a winner.'

'Yes, the more the merrier. I'll send you the details.'

'I'll see you then, Wil.'

After the call, Wil switched the lights off in the studio, locked up and walked to his car parked nearby.

Before getting into his car, he gazed up at the clear night sky filled with stars. And he thought about Delphie, wondering if she was working late in the barn. He had a strong urge to take her up on her invitation to paint, but it was too late in the evening. Another night, he told himself.

The next morning, Wil took a call from Callum.

'That was fast work, Callum. I'll come along now and pick up the paintings.'

It was another bright morning, and the shops along the main street, some with canopies, others with hanging flower baskets or bunting, looked lovely.

As he approached the art shop, Wil noticed another seascape painting by Callum was on display as he went into the art shop.

'Morning, Wil,' said Callum. The large foxtrot watercolour and set of three pen and ink drawings framed were on the counter ready for collection.

'You've made a great job of framing the artwork,' Wil told him.

'Delphie's watercolour is beautiful,' said Callum.

'She's incredibly talented.' Wil almost added about her dance skills, but decided to keep that to himself for the moment.

Wil paid Callum and picked up the paintings. 'I can't wait to hang them up.'

Delighted with his paintings, Wil left the art shop and headed to the dance studio.

Delphie was in the bakery shop, eyeing the selection of cakes. She'd only driven down to buy more paint from the art shop and stopped by the bakery on her way back to her car.

'Tea, please, Catriona, and I'll have a chocolate chip cupcake.'

Catriona poured a tea to go and bagged the cake.

Sienna happened to see Delphie through the bakery shop window and walked in, determined to force a conversation.

Catriona and Delphie were so busy chatting that neither of them noticed Sienna as she approached the counter.

'Do you want to treat Wil today?' Catriona said to Delphie.

Before Delphie had a chance to say that she hadn't intended seeing Wil today, Sienna interrupted.

'Mocha is Wil's favourite flavour,' Sienna said, taking Delphie aback.

Catriona didn't know Sienna and wondered what was going on.

Delphie tried to hide her surprise, glanced at Sienna and then ordered a cake for Wil. 'I'll take a strawberry cupcake for Wil.'

Catriona bagged the order, sensing the tension between Delphie and Sienna.

Delphie paid for the tea and cakes. 'Thanks, Catriona.' As she turned to leave, she commented to Sienna. 'Wil has a new favourite.'

Sienna glared at Delphie.

Without glancing back, Delphie left the bakery and walked away.

A call came through from Wil as she approached her car.

'I picked up the paintings this morning. They look great hanging up in the studio.' He sounded so happy.

'That's wonderful.' She was about to tell him about Sienna, then changed her mind as he continued.

'I've a really busy day ahead, but I just wanted to let you know.'

'I'm glad you like them, Wil. I've a busy day too, so I'll let you get on with your day.'

The call finished on a happy note.

Delphie sighed, got into her car and drove off home.

Later that day, Delphie painted in the barn while chatting to her grandmother on a video call on her laptop.

'How are you getting on with the paintings for Wil?' said her grandmother.

'Forging ahead,' Delphie told her.

'Wil sounds nice from what you've told me.'

'He is,' said Delphie.

Her grandmother gave her a knowing smile. 'Is that a spark of interest in him I see in you?'

'No sparks, except for the ones flying off my paintbrushes.'

'I looked him up online,' her grandmother confided. 'He's a marvellous dancer. And so handsome.'

'You're incorrigible.'

'And you need to move on from a broken heart. It'll mend so much quicker with new love in your life.'

'I have plenty of love for my art.'

'Well, keep your options open. Maybe do a painting of Wil. His posture and dance presentation are wonderful. Perhaps it would let you see him in a more romantic light.'

Delphie shook her head and smiled. 'I think the romance of Paris is turning you into a matchmaker.'

Her grandfather peered into view. 'This Wil guy reminds me of myself. Tall, handsome, a great dancer, romantic at heart.' He wrapped his arms around his wife and danced and hugged her playfully.

Laughing, they ended the video call on a cheerful note.

Delphie held her brush for a moment and thought about her grandmother's suggestion to paint Wil. Scrolling through her laptop to find pictures of him, she paused at one where he was in a strong but elegant dance pose.

Putting her brush aside, she started to sketch him on her drawing pad, unaware that she had a visitor.

'Knock, knock,' Wil said, standing in the wide open doorway of the barn. He wore a sky blue top. It fitted his physique, emphasising his trim torso, lean but muscular arms, broad shoulders and strong back. A dancer's top that suited him so well, worn with dark trousers.

Delphie jolted. 'Wil! I didn't expect to see you. I thought you had a busy day.' Guilt edged her voice and she tried to surreptitiously hide the sketch that was a fair likeness of him. No mistaking it was Wil.

'I cleared the work quicker than I'd anticipated. And thought I'd take you up on your offer of joining you to paint. Unless this is an inconvenient time.'

Delphie smiled tightly and hoped he hadn't caught a glimpse of the sketch.

But he had, and frowned as he walked over to her. 'Is that a new dance figure you're drawing?'

She closed the laptop, but he'd seen the picture of himself on screen too. 'It's nothing special.'

'He looks familiar,' Wil said, smirking.

'He's just a fictional interpretation of someone.'

'Really?'

Wil went to peek at the sketch, but Delphie closed the drawing pad. 'It's a rough sketch.'

'No one has ever painted me before.'

'Maybe they never will,' said Delphie.

'I don't mind. I'm flattered,' he assured her.

Delphie sighed and relented. 'Okay, but it was my grandmother's idea. I told her that I'm doing artwork for your dance studio. She thought you looked handsome.'

Wil stepped closer. 'What does the artist think?'

Delphie felt a blush form across her cheeks. She totally agreed with her grandmother, not that she intended telling him.

'Do I make a suitable subject?' he prompted her.

'Given the right light, the right pose,' she joked. 'You could make a fine figure to paint.'

Wil playfully struck an exaggerated pose. 'How about this angle?' Then another one. 'Or this?'

Delphie put a paintbrush in his hand. 'First lesson in learning to paint. Don't mess with the teacher.'

Wil stood to attention, smirked, and pretended to defer to Delphie. 'Where do I start?'

'Everything starts with a pencil drawing, but I think we'll skip the sketching and let you try painting with watercolours. Then acrylics for the next lesson.'

'I'll be invited back?' He pretended to be surprised.

'Only if you behave yourself.'

Wil shrugged. 'That's me thwarted then.'

Standing together at her artwork table, she started to show him basic watercolour techniques. 'We'll begin with letting you try to paint wet on wet.'

CHAPTER FOUR

'Perhaps I'm more of an oil painter,' said Wil, admitting defeat with his attempt at watercolour.

'Watercolour techniques take time to learn. You've done quite well for your first eight attempts.'

Wil laughed at Delphie's exaggeration.

'But next time, I'll let you have a go at painting with acrylics.'

'I'm up for that.'

He glanced outside. A golden hour glow shone into the barn. They'd both lost track of the time.

'I should go and let you get some proper artwork done,' he said.

'Your hands are covered in paint. Come over to the farmhouse to clean up before you go.'

Leading Wil outside and over to the farmhouse, she gazed up at the approaching twilight. 'The skies are beautiful here.'

'You should paint a night sky filled with stars.'

'I'm more of a people painter.'

'Add a couple dancing under the night sky,' he suggested.

Delphie liked that idea. 'That would look wonderful if I could capture the atmosphere of the stars and the twilight's glow.'

'Try. You're a talented artist.'

She loved the way Wil bolstered her confidence. It made her realise that none of the men she'd dated ever did that.

'The kitchen is through here,' she said.

Wil followed her and washed his hands at the sink. 'The watercolour washes off easily.'

'No one will ever know what you've been up to.'

He looked at the colourful splashes on his blue top.

'Though I should've let you borrow an apron to protect your clothes,' she said.

Wil brushed aside any concern. 'Proof that I gave my artistic urges a go.' Other urges surged through him. The urge to invite her to have dinner with him. To tell her how lovely she was and that he enjoyed being in her company. Instead, he dried his hands and got ready to leave.

'Are you heading back to the dance studio?'

'No, I thought I'd go home and work there, jot down ideas for choreography.'

'I'm going to make a light and easy dinner. You're welcome to join me.' Her heart raced as she found herself stepping into territory she hadn't intended.

For a moment, she thought he was going to say no, make some excuse, and part of her hoped he would. Then she wouldn't have to deal with the excited beating of her heart, and could have dinner and then work on her paintings again. A safe world. A world she could control without blushing and inviting feelings she'd been determined to ignore.

'On one condition,' he said. 'I help you cook dinner.'

'Deal.'

Wil smiled and looked around. 'What will we make?'

Delphie opened the well–stocked fridge. 'Luckily, I picked up groceries when I was in the main street earlier.'

Wil saw a jar of pasta in the kitchen, peered in the cupboards and began to take charge. 'I could make my special pasta. You have all the ingredients — plenty of tomatoes, peppers, herbs and spices.'

'You cook?'

'I live on my own. I eat out quite often when I'm busy, but I've learned to make a few dishes that are easy and tasty.'

Delphie washed her hands. 'What can I do to help?'

'Start cooking the pasta while I make the sauce.'

Working around each other, moving as if they'd been choreographed, they prepared dinner and sat down at the kitchen table to enjoy their meal.

'Mmmm, this is so tasty,' Delphie enthused.

Wil smiled at her, pleased she was enjoying it. 'I hope you'll come along to the opening night I'm having at the studio. I've invited a few dancers, and others from the industry.'

'When is it?'

'A couple of nights from now. Around seven.'

'Yes, I'll come along. Though I don't know if I'll have any other paintings finished and framed by then.'

'Don't rush your work. The paintings hanging up are wonderful. I keep admiring The Sweetest Waltz. It's my favourite. Oh, and I've added the wall of twinkle lights that you suggested.'

Delphie smiled, happy that he loved the painting and had used her idea for the lights.

After dinner, Wil got ready to leave. Delphie walked with him to the front door. They stood outside the farmhouse for a moment, breathing in the night air.

'Thanks for dinner,' he said.

'I hope your new choreography ideas go well tonight.'

'I'm planning a routine with a tango element. Do you tango?'

'I used to love it. It's so dramatic.'

Wil glanced at the barn aglow with twinkle lights inside. 'Could I persuade you to try the routine with me? Just once. It's easier with a partner.'

Delphie hesitated. 'My tango moves are a bit rusty.'

'I don't believe that for a moment. Come on, dance with me, then you can get on with your painting.'

Delphie glanced down at her flat pumps. 'I'm not wearing the right shoes.'

'I'll wait while you change into heels,' he said, looking content to stand in the evening air.

Delphie hurried inside the farmhouse and up to her room. She threw her jeans and shirt off, grabbed a dress, put it on and stepped into a pair of heels suitable for dancing.

Running outside to join him, Wil laughed when he saw her.

'That was quick.'

Delphie smiled and shrugged. 'I really do need to work on slowing down, but sometimes it comes in handy.'

Walking together over to the barn, Delphie pulled the sheet on the floor aside.

Wil scrolled through his phone to find the music he'd been rehearsing to, then set it down on the table to play.

'Ready?' he said, taking her in hold.

'What's the first move?'

'Follow my lead. It begins with a few traditional moves.'

They started dancing, slow, dramatic moves. Delphie followed Wil's lead, adjusting when the steps picked up pace.

The music resounded through the barn, rising in tone and tempo, and Delphie was swept along in Wil's routine.

She felt the lean muscles on his arms and shoulders as they danced together. The tension in his torso as he held her close to him. His strength was evident, but controlled, taking the lead in their tango.

'Excellent,' he said. 'Now turn, spin, then come back to me in close hold.'

Delphie instinctively danced the moves as he'd hoped, and they finished the piece of choreography face–to–face, their lips a breath away from touching.

Wil resisted the temptation to kiss her, and instead spun her away from him, as if finishing with a flourish.

Letting go of her hand, he heard the tension release in his voice. 'That's all I've choreographed. As I said, I'm still working on it.'

'I like the mix of staccato style with sweeping drama.' Her heart was still thundering from the experience. Dancing with Wil affected her in so many ways, but she told herself that it was the effect of the dance.

Running his hand through his hair to clear his thoughts, he stepped away and took a deep breath. 'I think the routine works up to that point. Thank you for indulging me.'

He picked up his phone, smiled and walked out to his car.

Delphie stood in the doorway of the barn and waved him off. An unexpected ache shot through her heart seeing him drive away. Sweeping aside any thoughts she had about becoming romantically involved with him, she walked over to the farmhouse to change into her comfy clothes. The night was wearing on, but there was still a couple of hours left before she'd go to bed. And the feelings he'd instilled in her needed to be worked off. She headed back over to the barn to work on her paintings.

Wil drove away and wished he hadn't danced the tango with Delphie. The feelings he'd been trying to suppress surged through him, putting his heart in jeopardy.

Delphie was so sweet, but when she danced the tango, he could feel the fire in her ignite.

Instead of driving home, he continued on to the studio. Dancing with Delphie had given him so many ideas for the choreography. He wanted to work on the moves, burning up the dance floor, searing off the excess energy and excitement she'd sparked in him.

Delphie let herself be distracted. Instead of working on the paintings in the barn, she sat down at her artwork table and opened the sketch pad where she'd drawn Wil.

She started to smooth the rough sketch into a finished piece of line art that she then used as a template to draw on to a canvas.

Inspired from dancing the tango routine with him, she added flair to the figure, accentuating the muscles in his arms and shoulders. Tapering down to his lean torso and long, lithe legs, she then added the chiselled features of his handsome face, and swept her pencil lightly to emphasise the sensual curve of his hair from his forehead.

Years of working as a graphic designer had given her the ability to draw and design quickly, sometimes with details or impressionist lines.

Stepping back to gauge the canvas that was propped up on an easel, she nodded to herself. She'd captured the beating heart of Wil. In the painting, she reminded herself swiftly.

Selecting the acrylic paint colours she needed, she prepared her palette and began to paint. She painted a background from her imagination, based on seeing him dancing in his studio, grounding him on the dance floor, while adding elements that hinted of his studio. But she kept it understated with neutral tones so that the focus of the painting was on the figure.

The sleeves of his white shirt were rolled up to reveal his forearms, and it was unbuttoned at the neck to expose a hint of his chest. The dark trousers were class personified.

The canvas was a large poster–size enabling her to create details on the figure. The angle of his face as he gazed up at his outstretched hand, as if reaching for the stars, was perfect to highlight Wil's blue eyes.

She painted fast, as if needing to express everything in a burst of creativity that took her well past midnight, when she decided to let what she'd painted dry and continue with a fresh eye in the morning.

Leaving the canvas on the easel, she turned out the lights in the barn and headed over to the farmhouse.

Wil was still dancing in his studio after midnight. The video cameras he'd set up for talking to other dancers and showing them choreography came in handy. He filmed himself dancing, and kept reviewing the footage, changing the steps to improve the routine.

Satisfied he'd achieved what he wanted, he switched the cameras and lights off and headed out.

Wil walked along to his car, checking his messages. He was surprised to see that he had several, all similar. One message from a dancer read: *Thanks for the invitation, Wil.* Another read: *Looking forward to seeing your new studio.* A third: *I'll be there with Gareth.*

Part of him was pleased that so many dancers were coming along to see his studio, but now he had to cater for all these extra guests.

Getting into his car, he glanced at the bakery shop that was closed for the night. Maybe Catriona and Kian catered for party events. He planned to talk to them in the morning.

Wil walked along from the dance studio to the bakery shop the next morning.

Catriona and Kian were at the counter and smiled when Wil walked in. It was fairly busy. Catriona was serving a customer.

'What can I get for you today, Wil?' said Kian.

'Do you cater for parties?' The slight desperation sounded in Wil's tone.

'Yes, what did you have in mind?'

'I'm having an opening night at the dance studio tomorrow. I invited several people. But one man wanted to bring someone else along, and I told him *the more the merrier...*'

Kian laughed. 'So it's going to be a lot merrier.'

Wil nodded and looked concerned.

'A buffet would be your best bet,' Kian advised him. 'We cater for parties and small wedding receptions.'

'I know it's short notice,' said Wil.

'It's fine. I'll arrange a buffet for around twenty or so guests.' Kian sounded as if this was easily doable.

'I have a kitchen at the back of the studio, and folding tables and chairs.' When Wil had leased the premises, some of the previous items used in the old community hall were still stored at the back.

Kian wanted to have a look so he could start planning. He spoke to his wife. 'Catriona, can you take care of things here while I go with Wil to the dance studio. I won't be long.'

Catriona smiled. 'Yes.' Then she continued to serve customers as Kian headed out of the bakery shop with Wil.

Bright morning sunlight created a warm glow in the farmhouse kitchen.

Delphie sat at the table eating breakfast. Beside her bowl of cereal topped with fresh fruit, she had her drawing pad and sketched dancing figures while she ate.

Kian stood in the dance studio admiring the artwork on the walls. 'I love your paintings, especially this couple waltzing together.'

'That's my favourite. Delphie painted all of them,' said Wil.

'Wow! She's really talented. I knew she was an artist, but these paintings are fantastic.'

'She's working on more paintings for me.'

'Do you think she'd paint something for the bakery shop?'

'I'm sure she would. Figures are her speciality.'

Kian nodded enthusiastically. 'I'll talk to her.' Kian then concentrated on the buffet plan. 'I take it that your guests are mainly dancers?'

'Yes, or those working in the dance industry.'

'I'll come up with a menu to suit various tastes, but I'll keep it light, sweet and delicious with a few savoury specialities.'

'You're making me hungry just thinking about it.'

'Catriona and I will come along and set up two of those long folding tables you showed me. You won't really need chairs. With a studio and floor like this, I'm betting there will be a whole lot of dancing going on.'

'Yes, I'm planning to create choreography for other professional dancers while I'm taking time away from the city.'

'It's always wise to take a break sometimes, to set your compass on the right path again,' said Kian. 'Catriona and I did that a couple of years ago, then we opened the bakery shop and we're loving it. Originally, we were both chefs working in a large restaurant in the city. That's where we met, fell in love and decided we wanted our own business.'

'It seems to have worked out well for you.'

'Yes, but we needed that break, to take time to breathe a little.' Kian smiled at Wil. 'It sounds like you need that too.'

'Do you ever miss the city?' said Wil.

Kian shook his head. 'The strange thing is, we both feel like we're from the town now. Like we've always belonged.'

'It's a nice town.'

Kian nodded. 'It's a town and community that welcomes people into the heart of it. Folk help each other.' Kian then turned the conversation back to Wil. 'So don't worry about the buffet. We'll take care of everything. You concentrate on your dancing.'

'I appreciate your help, Kian.'

Smiling, Kian left with a reassuring wave.

Breathing a sigh of relief, Wil then sat down next to his music system, put his dancing shoes on and began rehearsing a new routine he'd been dreaming about the previous night. Not a tango — a waltz. A romantic waltz.

Delphie was still drawing at the kitchen table when a call came through from Kian.

'I saw the dance paintings in Wil's studio. Would you consider painting something for the bakery shop?'

'Eh, yes, but I mainly paint figures, people,' she said.

'Wil told me that. I don't have a creative mind, but maybe you have an idea for something we could hang behind the counter to brighten things up.'

'I'll put my mind to it.'

'Okay, I have to push on. I'm planning a buffet for Wil's opening night. Apparently a load more people are turning up than he originally intended.'

'Wil has invited me,' she told Kian.

'Well, dress to impress. It sounds like it's going to be an exciting night.'

After the call, Delphie checked the bakery shop's website and saw exactly what she needed. Flipping to a new page on her drawing pad, she used the photograph of Catriona and Kian standing behind the counter to begin sketching a rough outline.

The composition of the piece started to take shape. If she could portray Catriona and Kian working together, the counter filled with cakes and delicious items from the menu, it would be a talking point when customers came in.

Smiling to herself, thinking how pretty it would look painted in pastel pink and bright primary colours, she concentrated on the two figures. Both of them wore aprons to match the theme of the bakery shop. It would be lovely to paint this, even though sketching all those tempting cakes put her in the mood for a cup of tea and a biscuit.

She sketched cupcakes swirled with vanilla and strawberry frosting, a large chocolate layer cake, wedges of carrot cake sitting in the display, sandwiches filled with crisp green salad ingredients, and a bowl of fresh fruit with pears, bananas, grapes and bright shining red apples.

Catriona's auburn hair and Kian's light sandy hair blended well in warm tones that looked great in the photograph and would be ideal to paint.

Delphie took the sketch and hurried over to the barn to find a suitable size canvas. She'd bought a load of canvases in bulk and stored them in the barn. Each one was a stretched canvas over a wooden frame. They didn't require framing and were ready to hang when painted.

She found the size of canvas she needed. Without going any further with her design ideas, she called Kian and told him what she had in mind.

'That was quick work, Delphie.'

'I checked the photos on your website and the idea sprang to mind. A painting of you and Catriona working at the counter, to hang behind the counter. It would be fun.'

Catriona was listening and chipped in. 'We know you're busy with Wil's paintings, but put us on your list.'

'I'll do that,' Delphie promised.

After the call, she started working again on Wil's paintings, hoping to finish at least one to add to his wall for his opening night, especially if his party was going to be extra busy.

The remainder of Delphie's day was a colourful flurry of painting and creativity, as was the following day, leading up to the excitement of the party night at the dance studio.

CHAPTER FIVE

Looking through her grandmother's wardrobes that were filled with dresses, Delphie picked out a ruby red cocktail–length dress. This hit all the right notes. Not too subtle, not too sparkly.

She wore the dress with dark heels, just in case she needed to dance. She didn't intend to, especially as there would be lots of other proficient dancers there.

The upstairs spare room had a view of the sea in the distance, glistening in the evening light. Delphie had spent many a day in there playing, trying on her grandmother's dresses, especially the ball gowns, pretending that she was a princess in a fairytale castle. Or performing a dance routine on stage.

Jewellery boxes brimmed with beads, bangles and brooches, cosmetic jewellery. Fashion accessories of the eras, now vintage in style, were kept in wooden boxes lined with velvet. Seeing them again brought back a rush of memories of all the happy times she'd had there.

Delphie checked her reflection in the full–length mirror, and phoned her grandmother. 'Hello, Gran. I'm borrowing one of your dresses.' She held the phone up to show her reflection.

Her grandmother smiled, delighted. 'Oh, you look a treat. Are you going to a party?'

'Wil invited me to an open night he's having at his dance studio. Other dancers will be there.'

'The red dress is perfect on you. Are you wearing your dancing shoes?'

'Heels.'

'Does Wil know that you can dance?'

'Yes, he was surprised,' Delphie said, underplaying his reaction. 'But I helped him practise a new tango routine in the barn.'

'Oooh! That sounds promising.'

'No, neither of us is looking for romance in our lives right now. We're just getting along in business and keeping things friendly.'

Her grandmother laughed.

'Really,' Delphie emphasised. 'I'm taking a couple of paintings I've finished to the studio. I took you up on your idea to paint Wil. I'll send a photo of it to you.'

'I'm sure he'll be thrilled.'

Her grandfather joined the conversation, smiling at Delphie. 'I thought I heard you two chatterboxes. Come on, our carriage awaits,' he added jokingly to his wife.

'We're off to a night out at the theatre again,' her grandmother explained quickly. 'Enjoy the party with Wil. And help yourself to the handbags in the drawers. There's a red sparkly clutch that would go nicely with that dress.'

'Thanks, Gran. And enjoy your night out too,' Delphie called to her grandparents before they ended the call.

Delphie opened the drawers and saw several clutch bags, two of them red, and opted for the sparkly one.

Picking up the clutch, she headed downstairs where she'd left the two paintings she'd finished for

Wil. The tango dancers and the portrait of him. Both were painted on canvas and didn't require framing.

Carrying the paintings out to her car, she felt butterflies of excitement at the thought of surprising Wil with the paintings, and meeting some of the dancers.

Wil wore an expensive suit, shirt and tie. The dance studio was aglow with lights, and Kian and Catriona had prepared a buffet that was set on two long tables at one end of the room. As guests could help themselves, they'd left Wil to handle the party himself.

He stood in the heart of the studio and welcomed the first guests of the evening, giving them a look around and discussing his plans to create choreography.

Later, Wil was standing in the reception when Delphie arrived armed with the artwork. 'I finished another two paintings.'

He hurried over to take charge of the paintings, eager to see them, and was taken aback that she'd finished his portrait.

'I know you don't have time to hang them up,' said Delphie.

'I didn't expect you to have finished the tango painting. It's gorgeous.' He sat it up behind the reception desk so it could be seen by guests.

'I'm pleased you like it. And the picture of you, well...it's sort of a little extra to wish you all the best for your new dance studio.'

Wil frowned at her. 'No, I intend buying it.'

Delphie shook her head. 'It's a gift,' she insisted.

He sat it up beside the tango painting and stepped back to admire them. 'Thank you so much, Delphie, especially for the portrait.' And then he looked at her. 'You look wonderful.'

She tried not to blush. She'd told herself she wouldn't, but a slight blush formed on her cheeks.

'Come on through and meet everyone.' Wil swept her through to where the guests were milling around and helping themselves to the buffet.

Brief introductions were made, and Wil was keen to tell them that Delphie had painted the artwork many of them had admired on the studio walls.

Delphie then tried to step aside so that Wil could mix with his guests, but he kept close to her, including her in the conversations about the studio and the choreography he planned to create. It was obvious that many of them assumed Wil and Delphie were a couple.

Everything was going well until one particular guest walked into the studio. Gareth stopped to chat with a couple of dancers, and hadn't yet seen Delphie or Wil.

Delphie gasped as soon as she saw Gareth and hid behind Wil.

'What's wrong?' Wil said, wondering what she was up to.

'Tango with me out to the reception,' Delphie said in a desperate whisper, trying to hide from Gareth.

Wil frowned round at her.

'Just do it, Wil,' she whispered urgently.

Wil took her in close hold and began to tango across the dance floor towards the reception.

Delphie pressed herself close to Wil. Their dramatic exit, although seen by most of the guests, bypassed Gareth as he was engrossed in conversation.

In the reception, Delphie stepped back from Wil as he released her from the tango hold.

He looked at her for a reasonable explanation.

'My ex–boyfriend is in there. He's one of your guests,' she told him.

'Which one?' said Wil, peering into the studio.

'The one with the burgundy shirt and waistcoat and a conceited smirk.'

Wil blinked. 'Gareth?'

'Yes.'

Wil felt his evening slide down a slippery slope.

'I didn't know he'd be here.' She got ready to run.

'Don't go, Delphie. I wasn't aware he was your ex. Gareth is merely an acquaintance I met through my dance work. He was the one who'd heard about my new studio. When he phoned I felt obliged to invite him. And then he asked if he could invite other dancers.'

'Gareth invited me,' Sienna announced, arriving in a fashionable black dress and heels.

The downward trajectory of Wil's evening slid even further.

Delphie looked at Wil for an explanation and found none.

'Gareth is auditioning suitable partners to dance with me,' Sienna said to Wil. 'Though I'm still hoping you'll reconsider and make us a winning twosome again.'

'I won't change my mind,' Wil said firmly.

His refusal didn't make a dent in Sienna's confidence. She glanced at her phone messages. 'Gareth says he's arrived. I know my way through.'

Leaving a trail of discord behind her, Sienna strutted through to the party.

Delphie clutched her bag and seemed ready to make a run for it.

Wil frowned at Delphie. 'I understand that you probably want to head for home, but I hope you'll stay here with me.'

The tone of his voice resonated through her impulse to bolt. Come on, she bolstered herself. You're not the type to run away from situations like this.

The expression on Wil's face showed that he wanted her by his side. Of all the nights. Both of them needed to back each other.

Delphie took a calming breath. 'What's the plan?'

'Walk back through and join the party. Or...' He stepped closer. 'Tango back in and make a real entrance.'

Delphie tucked her bag under the counter, then positioned her hands ready to tango.

The smile on Wil's face lit up her heart.

He took her in hold, but paused for a second to ask her something. 'Do you still have feelings for Gareth?'

'No.' Succinct, true.

Maybe she was reading too much into Wil's expression, but she was sure this news bolstered him.

Their tango didn't go unnoticed by Gareth, and as Delphie and Wil stopped and smiled in the centre of the dance floor, he was the first to approach them.

Gareth clapped and forced himself to look happy. 'Impressive moves, Wil.' Then his cool grey eyes focussed on Delphie. 'I hear you're Wil's new dance partner.'

'I'm enjoying working with Wil,' she said.

'Can I talk to you for a few minutes in private?' Gareth said to Delphie.

By now other guests had gathered around to chat to Wil. Not wanting to cause a scene, Delphie nodded and walked over to the buffet with Gareth.

Wil reluctantly watched her walk away.

'Is that the new tango choreography you're creating?' a guest said to Wil, sounding interested in discussing new routines with him.

'Yes, it's one of several routines I'm working on,' said Wil.

Another two dancers joined in the conversation, keen to plan ways to connect with Wil and learn new dance routines for contests and stage shows. As this was Wil's aim, he was pleased to discuss this with them, and soon found himself surrounded by several guests chatting about ways to develop choreography for them. But he kept glancing across at Delphie talking to Gareth. Seeing them together unsettled him. The unfamiliar feelings tearing through him made him realise he could so easily fall in love with Delphie.

Forcing the shields up around his heart, he concentrated on talking to his guests, making plans for when they could contact him via the online process he planned. He showed them the cameras he'd set up so he could train them remotely. Everyone was excited to work with him as he'd increasingly gained a reputation as an excellent choreographer. Splitting with his last two partners had an upside. He'd used the time to develop his choreography skills.

'You didn't return any of my calls,' Gareth said to Delphie as they stood at the side of the buffet.

'There was nothing left for us to talk about,' she told him bluntly. 'And there's still nothing.'

'I didn't handle things properly,' he admitted, keeping his voice down. 'I apologise for how I broke up with you.'

'Basically telling me you'd auditioned for a new girlfriend and I didn't get the lead role.' She heard the acid in her voice, but couldn't help feeling bitter.

Gareth moved close and gazed at her. 'If I could rewind time, I'd never have let you down or let you go.'

'Well, you did, so there's no turning back the clock.' She knew she was over him. He'd broken her heart so coldly. In the harshest of ways, it helped her to stop loving him. 'I've moved on with my life. I've found new happiness.'

The hurt and regret showed in the depths of Gareth's eyes. 'Would you ever consider giving me a second chance?'

She'd never sensed so much sincerity from him. And she knew him well. He wasn't the hearts and flowers type. Not a romantic at heart. But when they'd dated, she believed he had loved her. Now he was asking for another chance to put things right. Was she willing to take that risk? Or was she truly over him?

The answer Delphie gave herself took her aback as she cast a glance over at Wil. 'I could never love you again, Gareth.'

Like a dagger through his heart, from a dramatic scene from the many stage plays he'd been part of, he knew the curtain had come down between them.

His nod of acceptance of her decision was barely perceptible. 'Can we at least be friends? It's a big small world and I think our paths are bound to cross, our lives intertwining in dance, in art.'

Delphie tilted her head. 'Art?'

Gareth nodded slowly. 'As you know, I'm constantly auditioning dancers for stage shows and contests. But the stage shows are gearing up for the winter season. The cast, the costumes, everything is planned months in advance of the shows that will be in theatres for wintertime and Christmas.'

Delphie knew this. 'Yes, I understand.'

'That's one of the reasons I'm interested in working with Wil now, to start creating choreography for the forthcoming shows and events,' Gareth explained.

This made sense to her. 'But what does this have to do with art?'

'When I found out that Wil had a new studio here, I remembered you telling me that your grandparents owned a farmhouse in the town.'

'I'm looking after it while they're on holiday abroad.'

Gareth nodded as if he knew the details. No doubt some of this gleaned from Sienna.

'One of the shows I'm involved in requires a whole new concept for the stage production,' Gareth elaborated. 'It's a twist on a classic show with ballet and modern stage dancing. The theatre wants a fantastic poster, artwork to portray the beauty of the show. It's set in winter, with snow and magic and...they asked me to keep a lookout for an artist capable of capturing the theme. And I thought of you.'

'You want me to design the poster?'

'More than that. The art will be part of the show's theme. It'll be used at the front of the theatre, in the marketing and advertising of the show. And in the sets, the scenery. Your experience in dance, expertise as a graphic designer, and now as a painter...' He gestured to her painting of The Sweetest Waltz. 'You're the ideal artist to do this, Delphie. Say yes, or at least don't say no until you've considered it.'

This was the type of artwork task she'd often dreamed of. But working with Gareth? She didn't say yes.

'Think it over,' Gareth said calmly. 'Have dinner with me tomorrow night. I'm staying at the same hotel as Sienna.'

Delphie's eyes flashed at this news.

'Separate rooms. We're not dating. I've no intention of becoming involved with Sienna.'

Not that she cared about this. She didn't want to date Gareth herself. It was only the realisation of being able to trust Gareth, at least when it came to business.

Delphie hesitated.

'Please,' said Gareth. 'Just dinner. We'll talk. I promise not to pressure you. But you would be the best artist I know for this artwork design. I've been checking your website. I saw that you're selling your paintings online, and from the local art shop. And if you're planning to strike out on your own as an artist, not just a graphic designer, this would be a great way to launch your new career.'

It would. She knew it. Biting her lips to prevent herself letting slip how much she wanted to say yes, she continued to hesitate.

'Come on, Delphie. You were never one to back down from a genuine challenge. Say yes to having dinner with me.'

Delphie nodded.

From across the dance floor Wil saw Delphie agree to do something with Gareth. Their body language spoke clearly. Gareth had persuaded her to become involved in something she wasn't sure about. Another twist of the dagger went through Wil's heart.

'Is it true that you're Wil's new dance partner?' Gareth said to Delphie, clearly having his suspicions.

Before Delphie had a chance to reply, Wil came over to join them.

'Would you dance the tango routine we've been working on?' Wil said to her. 'A few guests are interested in seeing the choreography.'

Wil's request inadvertently answered Gareth's question.

'Yes,' Delphie said brightly to Wil.

Taking her hand, Wil led Delphie to the centre of the dance floor. Her red dress was perfect for the tango.

Everyone stood aside to give them the dance floor to themselves and were eager to see their performance.

'Remember the part where you turn and spin?' Wil whispered, getting ready to switch on the music.

Delphie nodded.

'Could you perform pirouettes, like you did before, ending over near the mirror?'

'Yes,' she confirmed. 'Where will you be?'

'I'll jump, turn and spin around the room, finishing near you,' he explained. 'Then we'll conclude in close hold. The way we did in the barn.'

Delphie remembered how she felt that night. The sparks of attraction. Now Wil wanted a repeat performance in front of an audience of experienced dancers. Would they sense the attraction? Or would they think that it was all part of the choreography routine?

Wil turned the music on, and took Delphie in hold. And they began to dance.

CHAPTER SIX

The atmosphere felt electric as Delphie and Wil danced around the room. The music resonated through the sound system, adding to the rhythm far more than when they'd danced in the barn listening to the tune on his phone.

There were times, Delphie thought, when everything felt just right for dancing, and this was one of them as the energy sparked with each move they made. It was as if they'd always been in tune, rather than only tried Wil's tango–theme choreography once before.

Wil admired Delphie's footwork, dancing in heels that were designed for fashion rather than such precision.

Between the staccato moves, they were face–to–face, with Wil gazing down into Delphie's eyes, adding to the drama of their performance.

Wil embellished parts of the tango, elevating the routine to a level that impressed the guests watching them.

When it was time for Delphie to perform her pirouettes, she spun like a ballerina, her red dress spiralling in waves of chiffon and silk dusted with crimson sparkles. The fire in her dance encouraged Wil to leap into the air, turn, land lightly and then jump again, spinning with strength and agility.

As Delphie neared the mirrors, Wil swept her into his last movement, and then they continued to tango to a triumphant crescendo, finishing with an almost kiss moment in the middle of the dance floor.

Applause erupted from the guests, and when Delphie blinked out of the bubble she'd been in, she saw all the smiling faces and heard the dancers clapping. Gareth joined in, raising his hands above his head to accentuate his praise for their performance. He'd seen Wil dance with Sienna a few times, including at live stage performances, but Delphie and Wil outshone the past as a new and exciting dancing couple.

Gareth glimpsed the resigned look on Sienna's face, and her applause was half-hearted. Any thoughts she still harboured to team up again with Wil were surely dashed on the rocks from the performance she'd just seen.

A couple of dancers that Wil had promised to train first, stepped forward, claiming that they wanted this routine.

'Could you choreograph something else with this type of tango vigour?' Steaphan, another professional dancer, said to Wil. Steaphan was in his early thirties with dark blond hair and blue eyes.

'Yes, I'll take a look at some of your latest performances and play to your strengths,' Wil told him.

'I don't have a partner at the moment,' Steaphan told him. 'But I'm planning to find one in a wee while.' He said it loud, hoping that maybe one of the guests would like to team up with him.

'I'm looking for a new partner,' Sienna told him. 'Would you like to take a turn around the floor?'

Steaphan's face lit up. He'd thought that Sienna, having been Wil's partner, wanted to reignite her success with Wil. But obviously she was now looking elsewhere.

'It would be my pleasure,' Steaphan said to Sienna, taking her hand and leading her on to the floor where others were now dancing, inspired by the tango performance.

'Gareth,' Sienna called to him. 'I need your thoughts on me dancing with Steaphan.'

Gareth stepped forward and nodded that he would give them his full attention. He hadn't considered Steaphan and Sienna as a match, but seeing them tango, he saw how well they danced together.

'Thank you for going along with my impromptu plan,' Wil said to Delphie.

She still felt euphoric from the experience. 'I love that routine.'

'I filmed us dancing,' he told her. 'I thought it would be fun to look back on.'

'I'm glad. I was so caught up in it, I'd love to view it,' said Delphie.

'I'll give you a copy to keep in your archives,' Wil added. 'A story to tell the grandchildren.'

Delphie laughed.

Wil looked mortified. 'What I mean is, if you should ever settle down and—'

Delphie cut–in. 'I know what you mean, Wil.'

He was still squirming but trying to smile.

'I love the stories my grandparents tell me,' said Delphie. 'I've learned so much from them, and continue to learn.' She swept her hands down her sparkly red dress. 'This is vintage, borrowed from my grandmother's collection of dresses that she wore when she was a dancer. There's a lot to be gained from the past.'

'Beautiful,' Wil's deep voice murmured, hinting that he wasn't just talking about the dress.

Delphie blushed, but ran her hands through her hair and said breezily. 'I think I'll have a cool drink from the buffet.'

'Mind if I join you?' said Wil.

Smiling at him, she walked over to the buffet where Wil poured them two glasses of fresh orange topped up with sparkling mineral water.

Delphie held her glass up. 'Cheers to you and your new studio.'

Wil tipped his glass against hers. 'Cheers.'

'What are you drinking a toast to?' Sienna said, interrupting them while Gareth chatted to Steaphan. 'Or is it a secret? Maybe planning to compete in the contest.'

'It is a secret,' Wil told Sienna, causing Delphie to blink. 'But we've no plans to enter the contest.'

Sienna drummed her long, well–manicured nails on her glass of wine. 'Perhaps not, but you're up to something. You've got that unsettled and mischievous look in your eyes. I could always read you so well.'

This was true, so Wil didn't try to correct her.

Sienna glanced at Delphie. 'Love your dress by the way. I had one just like it last season.'

The ice in Delphie's glass didn't rattle, even though Sienna rubbed her feathers up the wrong way. 'I doubt it. This is vintage.'

Sienna swallowed any further remarks, smiled and went over to join Gareth and Steaphan hoping they'd come to some agreement about the partnership.

'And vintage never really goes out of fashion, does it?' Wil said to Delphie.

'Nope. Even after all this time, it's still causing mischief.'

Wil put his glass down. 'Would you care to dance with me?'

Delphie placed hers aside too. 'I'd love to. What routine were you thinking of?'

'None. Just dance with me.' Taking her in his arms right there and then, he whisked her on to the dance floor.

In a whirl of excitement and fun, Delphie danced with Wil, another memory for the archives.

Wil's choice of music created a party atmosphere, and the evening became a resounding success as the guests enjoyed dancing everything from freestyle to classic foxtrot and cha–cha.

'This next song is ideal for a waltz,' Wil announced, encouraging everyone to take to the floor. They needed no encouragement, as almost everyone was up dancing.

'Mind if I cut in?' Gareth said, tapping Wil politely on the shoulder. 'I'd like to have at least one dance with Delphie.'

Unable to find an excuse to refuse without causing ructions, Wil smiled and stepped aside while Gareth claimed the next waltz with Delphie. It was a classic waltz that some would consider to be romantic, and as Gareth led her around there was an element of their past love that Wil caught a glimpse of as he stood and watched.

For the first time, Wil saw the couple they used to be. They probably looked like a suitable match, on the surface. And he admired Delphie, such an elegant dancer, looking like she might still belong in Gareth's world, especially as she was wearing a dress from the past.

Shaking these thoughts from himself, Wil was about to head over to the buffet when Sienna clasped his hand.

'Come on, Wil. We used to love waltzing,' Sienna said, encouraging him.

Letting himself give in to the moment, Wil waltzed around with Sienna in his arms. It served two purposes. One — it showed that they were excellent dance partners. Two — his heart longed to be with Delphie.

As the music changed to a slower beat, the evening finished with a romantic waltz.

Wil pried himself out of Sienna's grasp, wished her luck with her partnership with Steaphan, and claimed the last dance with Delphie.

Relieved to be back in Wil's arms, she nodded when Gareth said to her, 'See you for dinner tomorrow night.'

Gareth left the party, accompanied by Sienna.

Wil guessed this was what Delphie had agreed with Gareth. He didn't pry. It was none of his business why she had a dinner date with her ex–boyfriend.

Sensing the tension in Wil as they waltzed, Delphie told him about Gareth's offer.

'I agree with Gareth,' Wil found himself saying. 'With your talent as an artist, graphic designer, and background in dancing, you're the perfect person for the job.'

Delphie's emotions were split hearing Wil's reaction. Here he was, backing her to the hilt. But she wished she hadn't been put in this predicament.

'What's wrong?' Wil said to her, feeling her tense in his arms.

'Everything and nothing.'

Wil nodded as they continued to waltz slow and rhythmically around the dance floor. Under other circumstances, this would've been the perfect ending to a fun night. Instead, it felt like something that hadn't been given the chance to flourish had ended too soon. Dare he believe that there could've been a romance between him and Delphie? Was Gareth's arrival back on the scene something that would change what might have been?

'It's a wonderful opportunity to have your work recognised,' Wil told her. 'I'd heard a wee while ago that this show was being planned for the winter and Christmas. I was actually approached to dance one of the lead parts, but I'd already signed the lease on the dance studio, so I turned it down.'

'Maybe it was always on the cards that we would meet,' she said, hearing a hint of bittersweet in her tone.

'Sienna has asked me to have dinner with her tomorrow night at the hotel,' said Wil. 'She wants me to create a routine for her and Steaphan for the contest.'

'Dinner tomorrow night for both of us,' Delphie said, trying to sound chirpy.

Wil couldn't muster up a smile. 'Just not together.'

The music finished with a romantic flourish, and the guests curtsied and bowed to each other, concluding the evening.

'Great night, Wil,' a guest said to him. 'We'll speak soon about learning that new choreography.'

'Yes, call me in a couple of days,' said Wil. 'And send me your latest performances. I'll have a look at them and see what I can come up with for you.'

Giving Wil a broad smile, the guest and his dance partner left the studio.

Wil saw everyone out from the reception, and several commented on the tango painting and the portrait.

'I recognised you instantly, Wil,' one guest told him.

'Excellent work, Delphie,' another remarked.

Delphie was almost the last to leave. Collecting her bag from under the counter where she'd left it, she waved at Wil and headed out.

Wil was deep in conversation with two guests about choreography, preventing him from seeing her out, or talking to her about everything that had happened. He felt they needed to talk things through.

He heard the two dancers chatting to him about the type of moves they wanted to include in their routine. Moves that were their speciality. And yet, there was a moment of silence in him as he watched Delphie disappear into the night.

Blinking back into the conversation, Wil noted the moves the dancers wanted. 'I'm familiar with your past routines, and I'll bring a fresh approach to your choreography. I'll call you when I have an outline for your routine.'

Thanking Wil, they left him now standing all alone in reception.

Taking out his phone, he fought the urge to send a message to Delphie. Not even sure what he wanted to say. Something. Anything. But he pushed his foolishness aside, put his phone back in his pocket, and went through to tidy things up before heading home.

Finally turning the lights off in the studio, he stood for a moment in the glow of the light from the streetlamps shining in, and looked at his portrait. Is this how Delphie saw him? He was pictured strong and dramatic, and she'd captured the dance pose so well that he remembered when he'd danced this routine. Or was this just her artistic talent depicting him?

Sighing heavily, he locked up the studio for the night and headed out to his car.

Driving along the country road to his house, he wondered if Delphie was painting late into the night in the barn, or if she was sound asleep.

He pulled his car up in front of his house, got out and breathed in the heavy scent of the greenery and flowers. Gazing up at the sky, at the stars, he felt truly alone for the first time since he'd moved to the town.

As he walked across the garden, he took his phone out and sent a message to Delphie.

Thanks for not running away tonight.

He blinked as his phone lit up in the darkness with an instant reply from her.

Remember to send me a copy of our tango dance. Archives are important to me.

I will. I'll always remember our tango.

Goodnight, Wil.

Goodnight, Delphie. And thank you again for the portrait. I've hung it on the studio wall alongside the waltz.

Delphie clicked her phone off and continued to paint in the barn, lit by the lamps illuminating her artwork table. She knew how late it was. She was aware that she should've gone to bed and been sensible instead of burning the midnight oil. But some nights...well, that wildcard streak in her kicked in. Tonight was one of those times.

Obtusely, she took her time painting a quick step. Another painting for Wil. A couple more, and she would have completed everything he'd wanted. And he was under no obligation to buy all of them. She was quite happy to put the excess on her website for sale, or ask Callum if he was interested in selling them in the art shop.

But it was a fair bet that Wil would buy them all, and she'd deliberately tried to create a theme through them, whether they were acrylics or watercolours or pen and ink. The dance movements flowed, and the poses were as authentic as she could make them while retaining artist flair.

As she was steeped in thought, wondering if she should use Prussian blue and burnt umber to create the soft, muted tones she wanted for one of the paintings, she jumped when a call came through on her phone from her grandmother.

'Your grandfather said not to call this late at night, but I thought I'd take a chance that you'd still be painting.'

Delphie showed her what she was working on. 'I've got a production line going. And yes, I know I should be tucked up in bed but...'

'I wanted to let you see where we are.' Her grandmother held up her phone. 'We were at another show, and now we're taking a carriage ride through Paris.'

'Wow! It looks amazing.'

'We're scallywags,' her grandfather chipped in. 'I suppose being late night rascals runs in the family.'

Delphie laughed. 'I think it might have skipped a generation.'

Her grandfather guffawed. 'Oh, yes. Your parents wouldn't approve.'

'Definitely not,' Delphie agreed, giggling.

'I got the picture of Wil's portrait you sent,' her grandmother cut back in. 'It's a timeless classic. And he's sooo handsome. Did he love it?'

'He did,' Delphie said, sounding enthusiastic. 'He's hung it up alongside The Sweetest Waltz.'

'A fortuitous sign,' said her grandmother. 'And how did your red dress go down at the party?'

'Wil and I performed the tango, so it was the right dress for dancing.'

'I'd love to have been there to see that,' her grandmother said, sounding wistful.

'Wil has it on video. I'll send you a copy,' Delphie told her.

Her grandfather thumbed at his wife. 'She'll have me dancing it in Paris. You mark my words.'

'I most certainly will,' her grandmother confirmed. 'We're here to have fun, and dancing has been the joy of my life.'

'Ahem!' said her grandfather, causing them to laugh.

'Oh, and you too,' her grandmother said playfully.

Delphie didn't want to take the shine off their night, but she wanted to tell them about Gareth. She took a deep breath. 'Gareth was at the dance studio party.'

Her grandparents faces both appeared in view, blinking with surprise.

'Your Gareth?' said her grandmother.

Delphie nodded, and explained what happened.

'Don't let him wangle his way back into your affections,' her grandmother advised her. 'Unless you're still in love with him.'

'I'm not. And seeing him again confirmed I'm over him,' said Delphie.

'So you're having dinner with Gareth at the hotel restaurant,' her grandfather wanted to clarify. 'And Wil is dining with Sienna.'

'That's right,' Delphie told him.

'Romance can be awfy complicated,' he said, and then put his arm around his wife and hugged her close. 'I'm so glad we found each other and didn't need to jump through all those hoops of romantic fire to find our true love.'

'Be careful not to get scorch burns,' her grandmother warned her kindly, tucking into her husband's warm embrace.

'I'll be careful,' Delphie promised. 'But I don't know whether to take on the task of designing the artwork for the stage show.'

'I don't want to sway you,' said her grandmother. 'But if it was me, and I love that ballet, and how that'll be portrayed on stage in the winter, I'd grab the chance. It could help boost your career as an artist.'

'I'm really tempted to do it,' said Delphie.

'Then do it,' her grandmother told her. 'You don't need to fall back in step with Gareth. And if Wil's the type of man I think he is, it could all work out for the better.'

'Thanks for the advice,' said Delphie. 'Now I'm going to let you two night owls enjoy your ride around Paris.'

Her grandfather waved to Delphie.

'Remember to send us the tango video,' her grandmother managed to say before they ended the call.

Smiling to herself, and feeling better having spoken to her grandparents, Delphie continued to paint, thinking up ideas for the show's poster and graphic designs.

CHAPTER SEVEN

Wil knew the water would be brisk, but the sparkling silvery sea enticed him to go for a morning swim.

He'd parked his car on the esplanade, then walked down to the shore clasping a rolled up towel, and wearing a pair of swimming trunks under his clothes, eager to take Delphie up on her suggestion to enjoy the seaside.

A well–worn pathway, edged with grass and wild flowers, meandered to the shore and opened up to show a vista of light golden sand that stretched for miles along the coast.

The sea was calm, with barely a ripple on the surface. He imagined there would be blustery days when the waves would wash vigorously on to the shore. But this morning, beams of dazzling sunlight glistened across the sea, and he shielded his eyes as he gazed far into the distance, noticing a couple of white hull yachts with brightly coloured sails heading along the horizon.

He had a whole patch of shore to himself, so he shrugged off his shirt and trousers and left them on the sand beside his shoes and towel while he walked towards the sea. The sand beneath his feet felt great and the mild sea breeze gave no hint of how cold the water would be.

Wading in, he soon became accustomed to the brisk temperature, but it felt refreshing, so when he was thigh deep in it, he took the full plunge.

Submerging, he quickly resurfaced, unable to wipe the smile off his face.

Then he started swimming along part of the coast, keeping level with the shore, before turning around and doubling back to where he'd started.

Striding out, dripping wet, he felt invigorated, as if he'd had a workout and fun at the same time. Wil was fit, and his dancing kept him limber, but adding a swim to his schedule was something he planned to continue until the lingering summer weather turned colder. And maybe then he'd still go for a swim.

Picking up his towel, he dried off and then draped it around his shoulders while he stood on the shore breathing in the fresh sea air. The yachts had disappeared into the silvery yonder, and pale sunlight peered out from the awakening blue sky.

He'd had a late night and an early morning, and it was weighing on his mind about his dinner date with Sienna, and Delphie's date with Gareth. How quickly things had become complicated.

Shrugging off his concerns, he got dressed and walked back up to his car and drove home to shower and have breakfast.

Delphie sprinkled a handful of fresh raspberries on her breakfast cereal and sat at her kitchen table planning her day. Fully stocked with food, she didn't need to venture to the main street for groceries, so she was free to spend the whole day at the farmhouse and the barn working on her paintings.

Staying at the farmhouse still felt like being on holiday, but with every day that passed, she was starting to feel like she was home. The traditional, rambling farmhouse was large enough to make room for one more.

Her grandparents had often said she was welcome to stay with them for as long as she wanted. Until now, this hadn't been practical due to her work in the city. This thought brought up the offer she was due to discuss with Gareth over dinner. It jarred her. Was she stepping right back into the melee of work that she was trying to unwind from? Probably. But having slept on it, the opportunity still appealed to her.

Eating her breakfast, she decided to keep her options open and hear what Gareth had to offer at their dinner date.

After showering and making himself scrambled eggs for breakfast, Wil drove down to the dance studio to get on with his day.

He had new routines in mind and wanted to try out the choreography, but first, he downloaded the tango footage from the previous night and sent a copy to Delphie.

Wil phoned her as he pressed send. 'I've given you a copy of our tango,' he told Delphie when she picked up.

'Wonderful. I promised my grandparents I'd send a copy to them.'

'I think they'll be impressed with your dancing. You nailed every move, even the last minute pirouettes.'

'I had a great partner. But it was one of those nights when I felt that everything was just right.'

'It was,' he confirmed, holding back from telling her the fire he sensed in her when they danced.

'Are you working on new dance choreography today?' she said. 'A lot of your guests last night seemed eager for you to create routines for them.'

'Yes, that's my plan. I just wanted to make sure I gave you the tango video before I start work. And I took you up on your suggestion to make the most of the shore. I went swimming early this morning.'

'Brrrrh!' She shivered. 'Was it brisk?'

'Invigorating,' said Wil.

Delphie laughed. 'I really only meant for you to take a walk along the shore, enjoy the fresh sea air.'

'You might have clarified that,' he chided her lightly.

'But you seemed keen to go swimming, so I didn't want to dampen your enthusiasm.'

'I'm aiming to go again before the weather turns colder and too wild. Care to join me one morning?'

The hesitation from Delphie made him laugh. 'Ah, so it's okay for me to take a dook in the cold sea while you're all cosy in your farmhouse.'

'I'll think about it,' she said in a non–committal tone.

'That's not a no,' he said brightly. 'But don't hesitate for too long. You know how changeable the weather is in Scotland. We're heading into the autumn fast. I want to enjoy the warmer days before the winter seasons kick in. Though I'm certainly planning to take a dip when spring comes around again.'

'I'll be long gone by then,' she reminded him. 'I won't even be here by the time it's winter.'

His heart felt like it had taken a hit. 'I keep forgetting that you're on a different schedule. I'm here for a year. I need to remind myself that you're going back to Edinburgh when your grandparents come home.'

She did too. When she was with Wil, it was hard not to think that they were both in town for quite a while.

'My grandparents phoned me last night. They're having such a romantic time in Paris.'

'Maybe they'll extend their holiday,' he said hopefully. 'Or encourage you to stay a little longer in the farmhouse when they come home.'

'This was never my plan. That's why I'm going to hear what Gareth has to offer regarding the artwork for the stage show. When I go back to Edinburgh, I'm going to need art and design assignments.'

'Of course,' he agreed. 'You have to be practical about your career, though I think you have real talent to sell your paintings.'

'That's what I'd like to do. And the publicity from being the stage show's graphic designer could help boost my career.'

'It could,' he agreed, not wanting to dissuade her. 'But you could always come back to the town at a later date.'

'Yes,' she said, sounding as if she didn't believe she would.

'Well, I'd better push on with my day and let you get on with yours.'

'Thanks for the tango video, and I'll think about taking you up on your offer of an invigorating swim,' she said.

'I hope your dinner meeting goes well with Gareth,' he told her.

'And yours with Sienna.'

After the call, Wil sat down at the side of the studio, put his dance shoes on and tried not to feel like he'd let something precious slip through his fingers.

Turning on some lively music, he worked off his doubts with dancing.

Ideas for the poster's artwork kept interrupting Delphie's day. While working on the paintings, she'd stop and sketch designs that sprang to mind. It made her day go in quickly, and she spent most of it painting and drawing in the barn.

Grabbing a sandwich for lunch, she'd then worked on until it was time to get ready for dinner with Gareth.

There was nothing in her grandmother's wardrobes that she felt was suitable for having dinner in the restaurant. Flamboyant or fashionable? She opted for the latter, and found it in her own cache of clothes. A dress she'd worn for business meetings that spilled into social evenings.

Not quite cocktail, the dress had enough flair to boost her confidence when she faced–off with Gareth. Knowing him, he'd have planned a counter move for every objection she could think of. It was part of his job to bring ideas to fruition, so he was more experienced than she was when it came to making deals.

She wore the sapphire blue dress with heels that she was prepared to dig in if Gareth tried to sweet talk her into a deal she didn't want.

The day had been warm and sunny, but as Delphie drove down to the hotel at the far end of the main street, thunderclouds filtered out the amber glow of the sunset.

When she stepped out of the car, the sky arched above the traditional, family–run hotel, and the clouds seemed to be picking up pace as she walked towards the entrance.

A warm welcome was always guaranteed, and although Delphie hadn't dined there for a few years, she anticipated a delicious dinner. They specialised in Scottish and homely hospitality, and she was greeted with smiles and shown to her table as she walked through the reception to the restaurant.

Gareth was already seated at their table, and stood up to welcome Delphie.

'I'm glad you decided to have dinner with me,' he said. He looked particularly suave in a classic dark suit, but his shirt and tie had a dash of fashionable flair. Under other circumstances she would've admitted that Gareth was a handsome man, but she didn't want to let her resolve slip. Getting involved with her ex wasn't in her plans.

They were offered glasses of wine while they perused their menus, but they declined, preferring soft drinks. Delphie was driving, and she wanted to keep a clear head in case she needed to cross verbal swords with Gareth. He joined her in a refreshing fruit juice beverage.

Their polite chatter continued while their dinner was served. Delphie ordered rumbledethumps for her main course. A hearty dish made with mashed potatoes, turnip and cabbage, topped with Scottish cheddar cheese and greentails.

Gareth opted for salmon with neeps and tatties. The serving of turnip and potatoes was accompanied with a rich, buttery sauce.

The restaurant was fairly busy with most tables occupied. A table was reserved for Wil and Sienna.

Gareth began his pitch to Delphie as they ate their meal. 'I've sent you a copy of the previous poster that the theatre used for their festive show last year.'

Delphie paused and checked her messages, and there it was. 'I remember seeing this advertising the production, though I didn't manage to see the show.'

'We were both busy with work last Christmas.' He shrugged resignedly. 'We probably should've made more time for fun.'

Delphie nodded. 'And here we are, having dinner while discussing business. How long are you staying at the hotel?'

'A few more days. I really do want Wil's help to choreograph routines for some of the dancers I'm working with.'

'I love his choreography.'

Gareth picked up on Delphie's enthusiasm. 'Are you involved with Wil?'

'If you mean romantically, no.'

It was what he meant. 'I've seen the way he looks at you.'

Delphie concentrated on her meal, reluctant to meet Gareth's gaze. He was the shrewd type and could often read her well.

Before Gareth could pry further, Wil and Sienna arrived and were shown to their table.

Wil and Sienna nodded over to Delphie and Gareth, and they all acknowledged each other.

Wearing an expensive suit, shirt and tie, Wil looked handsome, and Delphie felt her heart react when she saw him.

Sienna wore a sleek black designer dress and exuded an air of confidence.

'Is Sienna dancing in the show?' Delphie said to Gareth.

'It's undecided. We're concentrating on the contest.'

'Do you think Sienna has a chance of winning?'

'Yes, if she'd been partnered with Wil. Maybe now that she's dancing with Steaphan. It'll depend on whether Sienna can convince Wil to create their routine. That's what they're discussing over dinner.'

Delphie glanced across at them, unable to read whether they were getting along well or at odds.

As if sensing her, Wil looked over at Delphie, and for a moment they connected before Delphie continued her conversation with Gareth.

'I sketched some ideas for the poster,' said Delphie. 'Not that I'm saying I'll tackle the artwork, but...'

'Can I have a look at the sketches?'

She dug out her sketch pad from her bag and handed it to him.

Gareth smiled, put his cutlery aside and had a look at her drawings.

'They're rough,' she said. 'I sketched them while I was painting in the barn.'

'These are terrific. I love the stars and the snow, the feel of winter, Christmastime from the past.'

'I wasn't sure if you were aiming for something more modern.'

'No, this is the type of atmosphere audiences will love. The past, nostalgia, is what I've been discussing with the show's director.'

'Once the two lead dancers are announced, their photograph would fit into the design,' said Delphie.

Gareth shook his head. 'No, seeing the dance figures you've been painting, I'd want you to paint them. That's why I said it would really help to promote your artwork.'

The conversation continued into the different details needed for the designs.

By the time their desserts were served up, Delphie had agreed to take on the task.

'I'll have an agreement drawn up and we'll work out a deadline schedule,' said Gareth, lifting up his glass. 'Cheers.'

'Cheers,' said Delphie.

Wil was listening to Sienna talk about her plans for the contest, but he couldn't help but notice the obvious agreement toasted between Delphie and Gareth. She'd taken on the artwork assignment.

'So I'll come by the studio tomorrow afternoon with Steaphan and Gareth to try those moves for the routine,' said Sienna.

Wil nodded and ate his dinner.

Delphie and Gareth had both ordered cranachan, a delicious mix of rich cream, raspberries, a dash of whisky, honey and oatmeal. They tucked into their desserts and discussed details for the artwork, and dancing.

'I'm planning to talk to Wil about having him create choreography for Sienna and Steaphan,' Gareth told her. 'We're meeting him at his studio. Will you be there?'

'No, I'll be up at the farmhouse, painting.'

'I thought you'd be at the studio, rehearsing your dance routines with Wil. Your tango was amazing. What else are you planning?'

Wil had walked over to their table and overheard the latter part of their conversation.

'A romantic waltz,' Wil said, cutting–in on their conversation. He smiled at Delphie urging her to agree with him.

'Yes,' said Delphie. 'A sweet, romantic waltz.'

'I'd love to have a look at that,' Gareth said, sounding interested.

'We'll give you a peek tomorrow,' Wil told him.

Gareth frowned. 'Delphie said she wouldn't be at the studio.'

'I'll pop down for a wee while,' Delphie confirmed.

Wil smiled tightly. 'I wondered if you'd both care to join us for a drink after dinner.'

'Yes,' said Gareth.

Delphie nodded.

Wil went back to his table, and Sienna continued her conversation about what type of routines she wanted Wil to create for the contest without missing a beat.

'Steaphan's strengths are in his dynamic moves. That's where we could both shine.' Sienna gestured to emphasise her intent. 'I want our choreography to explode on the dance floor.'

'No slow romantic waltz elements.'

Sienna brushed even the thought of this away. 'No, it needs to be powerful and potent.'

'Few things are more powerful and potent than love and romance,' he argued.

Sienna countered this with a flat no. 'I want dynamic drama.'

'Noted,' Wil said, already having some moves in mind.

Sienna glanced over at Delphie and Gareth deep in conversation. She leaned forward and spoke in a confiding tone to Wil. 'I'm sensing a reconnection between the two of them. I hope you won't end up without a dance partner again.'

Wil's outward response clashed with his true concerns. 'Delphie wouldn't do that to me. Besides, Gareth works auditioning dancers, helping to manage them. He's not a dancer.'

Sienna dropped a piece of news that took Wil aback. 'He used to be. Gareth danced all over the world.'

Wil leaned back in his chair. 'I didn't know that.'

'Gareth doesn't fanfare his past. But that doesn't mean he can't dance rings around others if he needed to.'

The only rings that Wil was concerned about were the ones where Gareth was circling his way back into Delphie's heart.

Wil surreptitiously sent a message to Delphie.

Don't worry about the romantic waltz. We can show them some standard waltz moves.

Delphie glanced over at Wil as she replied. *Okay.*

While they all finished having dinner, a live band set up on the small stage at the far side of the restaurant's function room that included a dance floor.

One of the hotel's owners came over to Delphie and Gareth's table. 'We're having a ceilidh night, Delphie. I hope you'll be up giving it laldy. You were always a fine wee dancer.' Smiling and meaning well, she hurried away to entice Wil and Sienna to take part. As Sienna and Gareth were guests, the hotelier knew they were into their dancing. And local gossip ensured they'd heard about Wil and his studio. Having four wonderful dancers in their restaurant was an opportunity not to be missed.

Delphie stared at Gareth. 'Did you know this was a ceilidh night?'

Gareth's expression matched his denial. 'I'd no idea.'

It was then that Delphie noticed a poster on the wall advertising an evening of dinner and dancing.

The live band of two fiddle players and an accordionist, started to tune up.

Delphie looked over at Wil, feeling her uneasy expression matched his.

'Shall we join Wil and Sienna?' Gareth stood up and smiled at Delphie.

Delphie sensed trouble brewing. They weren't obliged to join in with the ceilidh, but she had a feeling that the night was about to kick off with a bit of a Scottish stooshie.

CHAPTER EIGHT

'I don't do ceilidh dancing,' Sienna said when Wil suggested they join in. Lively music played and people were up joining in.

'It's just for fun,' Wil told her. 'I'll help to keep you right.'

Sienna folded her arms across her chest and sat at their dining table. 'I'll watch. You jig, twirl or whatever.'

The hotel owners waved at Delphie, encouraging her to enjoy the dancing. Hearing the music and seeing the guests give it a go, some experienced, others just up for a happy time, Delphie felt the urge to join them.

'I love a ceilidh,' Gareth said, eager to burn off some energy on the floor.

Accompanied by Wil and Gareth, Delphie headed over and the three of them joined in a reel. They linked arms with each other and soon they were part of the reel, whirling and twirling with other guests before making their way back together.

Despite everything that had happened with the arrival of Sienna and Gareth in town, throwing her plans to the wind, she found herself laughing and enjoying the ceilidh, letting go of her concerns, and just having fun.

Gareth and Wil arched their arms while Delphie danced underneath, and then they all linked hands in the fast–moving circle, whooping and cheering.

Wil lifted Delphie off her feet as he spun her around, causing her to burst out laughing. And then

Gareth did the same before she could hardly catch her breath.

It would be the genuine laughter and fun of the dancing that Delphie knew she'd remember from this night. The evening they'd started out dining at separate tables. Now they were indeed giving it laldy on the dance floor as one dance merged into the next with barely a beat of a pause. To call it lively was an understatement, but the live band were excellent and rose to the occasion.

Perhaps it was seeing Delphie have so much fun with Wil and Gareth that encouraged Sienna to step on to the floor.

Before she'd even had a chance to announce to them that she'd decided to join in, she was pulled into the heart of it and was soon smiling along with the others.

As an expert dancer, Sienna found her footing fairly well, and there were times when, like Delphie, her feet barely touched the floor.

Delphie and Sienna performed an impromptu fling while Wil and Gareth clapped to the beat, before the foursome joined hands and whirled around.

Their dancers' flexibility, fitness and flamboyance all came into play.

They finally stepped off the dance floor and went back to their table for a refreshing drink.

Gareth sat back in his chair and pretended to be totally puffed out.

'You're fit as a fiddle, Gareth,' Wil said, having none of his nonsense.

Gareth guffawed. 'That was fun. I love a challenge.'

'You should try an early morning swim in the sea,' said Wil. 'I did, at Delphie's prompting. And I'm trying to persuade her to join me for a brisk dook down the shore.'

'I'd be up for that,' Gareth confirmed. 'I'm guessing it's brisk and breezy.'

'Oh yes,' said Wil. 'Combine that with tonight's ceilidh dancing and I'd say I've had a lively day.'

Gareth took a deep breath. 'Okay, Wil, you've talked me into it. Flippers and snorkels at dawn tomorrow.'

Wil laughed. 'I'll pick you up at the hotel in the morning. All you need is your trunks.'

'Are you going to join us?' Gareth said to Delphie.

She almost choked on the iced drink she was sipping. 'I'll take a rain check.'

Sienna took them aback as she piped up. 'I'll go. I love to swim.'

'The sea is a bit cold,' Wil warned her with a smile.

Sienna flicked her hair back. 'I'm fine with that. Unless you're not up for me joining in.'

'No, you're welcome to come along,' said Wil. 'I'll pick both of you up in the morning.'

All eyes turned to Delphie, and she knew her resolve would wane. 'Okay, but be warned. The only swimsuit I have with me is neon pink. If you've got sunglasses, wear them,' she joked.

The light-hearted banter between them dissolved any tensions for the remainder of the night.

Delphie sensed it was the cheery calm before the storm, but decided to make the most of it. More ceilidh dancing was enjoyed and it was late in the night when they all finally parted ways.

Gareth and Sienna headed up to their rooms in the hotel, while Wil walked Delphie to her car that was parked near his.

'Are we really going to do this?' Delphie said standing for a moment in the night air.

'Oh, yes.'

She checked the time. 'I was supposed to be unwinding here in the town. Now I'll be grabbing a few hours sleep and then swimming in the sea at the crack of dawn.' She frowned jokingly. 'I must've got my plans mixed up. Now I'm thinking I'll need to head back to the city to relax.'

'It's not the location, it's the company you keep,' he said.

'Then you're a bad influence on me, Wil.'

'Bad to the bone,' he said with a smile and walked over and got into his car. Opening the window he called to her. 'Is your swimsuit really neon pink?' He wondered if she was joking.

'Yes, be prepared to be dazzled.' Delphie drove off, leading the way along the main street and up to the country road. Wil followed her.

Flashing his headlights, Wil peeled off when he reached his house as she drove on the short distance to the farmhouse.

What a night it had been, she thought. She'd expected tension and drama. Instead she'd danced at the ceilidh, and now she had to fish out her swimsuit from her luggage ready for the morning mayhem.

In the early morning sunlight, Wil drove down to the hotel, having sent a message to Gareth that he was on his way.

Wil frowned when he saw three figures waiting to be picked up for the swimming trip. Sienna was there with Gareth, but standing beside them was Steaphan. The more the merrier expression crossed Wil's mind, but he quickly discarded it, remembering how that had worked out the last time.

He pulled up and Sienna got into the front passenger seat beside him, while Gareth and Steaphan sat in the back.

'Steaphan's staying at the hotel,' said Sienna. 'When I told him we were going swimming, he wanted to join us.'

'I don't have swimming trunks, but I've got a pair of training shorts to wear,' Steaphan explained.

'That's what I'm wearing too,' Gareth added. 'I didn't think I'd be going swimming when I packed.'

'I only brought dancewear and fashion items,' said Sienna. 'But I'm wearing a black leotard that I'm sure will be fine.'

'Is Delphie still joining us?' Gareth said to Wil.

'She hasn't contacted me since last night,' said Wil. 'But I don't think she's the type to back down from a challenge.'

By now they we'd reached the nearby shore, and discarding their outer clothes, they viewed the sea. They had it all to themselves.

Sienna shivered and did a few warm–up moves.

'Here's Delphie now,' Wil said, seeing her car driving along the shore road.

For easiness, she'd worn a shift dress and pumps, and quickly took them off in the car and stepped out ready to join them, noticing that Steaphan was there too.

Wil pretended to shield his eyes against the glare of her pretty pink swimsuit.

Delphie swiped at him playfully.

Gareth rubbed his hands together. He had a fit build, as did Steaphan, but it was Wil's lean, muscular physique that made Delphie's heart beat faster. She tried to focus on the sea, wondering just how cold it would be. Seeing Sienna shivering, wearing the black leotard that enhanced her model–like figure, did nothing to bolster her confidence. The sea looked fairly calm but cold. The breeze wafting along the coast had a bit of a bite to it, as if declaring that autumn was well on its way.

'I swam along the shore that way,' Wil announced. 'I continued for a wee while and then headed back.'

'That sounds fine to me,' said Gareth.

Steaphan nodded and stretched his lean muscles.

Wil smiled at Delphie. 'If we get lost, we'll use your swimsuit as a marker.'

'What if I swim underwater,' Delphie countered playfully.

'Unless you dive to the seabed, that pink glow will shine through the surface,' Wil joked with her.

Without further chatter, they all walked across the sand and waded into the sea.

Gasps as the cold water enveloped them, were soon replaced with determined smiles as they became acclimatised to the temperature.

Wil led the way, with Sienna keeping up beside him. Behind them was Gareth. Delphie swam steadily in Wil's wake with Steaphan alongside her, smiling.

'It's not as chilly as I thought it would be,' Steaphan called over to Delphie. 'It's refreshing.'

'Yes,' Delphie lied.

Seeing her new dance partner pay all his attention to Delphie, Sienna changed course and swam alongside Steaphan.

By now, Delphie had become accustomed to the sea. Remembering how she used to love spending the day down the shore, she felt invigorated and swam on to join Wil. He'd been keeping an eye on her in case she needed him, but clearly she was a capable swimmer.

Wil smiled over at Delphie. 'I think we should head back now.'

They'd swam quite a distance, and she nodded in agreement. 'Yes, but this is fun.'

Turning in tandem, they led the others back towards their starting point.

And that's when the racing challenge began. Starting with Steaphan wanting to take on Gareth.

Gareth was up for the challenge, but egged Wil to join in. 'Come on, Wil, we'll race you back.'

The calm surface of the sea became a surge of white waves as the three of them powered through the water.

Delphie's money was on Wil, though Gareth was a close second and obviously a strong swimmer. Steaphan wasn't entirely out of the running, but it was a two–man race to the finish.

Sienna was now swimming in line with Delphie. They weren't racing, but neither of them wanted to lag behind, so as Wil pipped Gareth in the challenge, the men watched Sienna and Delphie head for home.

Although Sienna was an excellent swimmer, Delphie's determination won through.

There were cheers all round and playful splashing as they all eventually waded out of the sea.

Delphie wrung the water from her hair and smiled at Wil. 'You're definitely a bad influence.'

Wil shrugged his broad shoulders and grinned at her, setting her heart alight.

They walked back to the cars and grabbed their towels to dry off.

Gareth fetched his phone from Wil's car and snapped a few pictures. 'No one will believe we actually did this. So smile,' he said, taking a group photo.

Sienna then wrapped her towel around herself and was the first to get back into Wil's car.

There was no heat yet in the early morning sun, so none of them lingered on the shore.

'See you later at the studio, Delphie,' Gareth called over to her before getting into the back seat of the car with Steaphan.

'Yes,' Delphie confirmed and then got into her own car.

Following Wil's car back to the main street, Delphie continued on heading home to the farmhouse, while Wil dropped the others at the hotel.

After showering, Delphie made herself a bowl of porridge for breakfast, and then went over to the barn to work on her art.

Images of Wil swimming down the shore kept interrupting her concentration. Under other circumstances, she might have let herself fall for him. But their lives, although currently entwined, would soon unravel when their careers took them in different directions. But she'd enjoyed her morning swimming with him and the others.

As the day wore on, a message popped up on her phone from Gareth.

See you soon at the studio. And here are a couple of pictures from our swim.

Delphie looked at them all standing together on the shore, smiling happily.

Another memory for the archives.

Wil practised dance routines in the studio to show Gareth, Sienna and Steaphan. They were due to arrive soon. But since his morning swim, he kept thinking about Delphie and he was particularly looking forward to seeing her.

Delphie put on her dancing shoes that had mid–high heels and t–bar straps. Their neutral tone blended with her deep blue dress. The classic bodice fitted comfortably, and it had cap sleeves and a lightweight skirt with a slight flair, ideal for dancing.

Gareth and the others had only just arrived at the dance studio when she walked in, following the sound of the upbeat music to find Wil demonstrating an opening move for a new routine.

Sienna wore another black dress and black shoes similar in style to Delphie's heels.

Although they all acknowledged Delphie's arrival, Wil continued to demonstrate the moves, and then danced with Sienna before partnering her with Steaphan and adjusting their opening stance.

'You wanted drama,' Wil reminded Sienna. 'This is a bold opening, so exaggerate the hold and lean back into a strong frame when Steaphan leads you across the floor.'

Gareth came over and stood beside Delphie at the side of the studio as they watched them practise. She saw her reflection in the mirrors opposite, but felt nothing seeing herself next to Gareth. All the love had gone, at least on her part.

The music had a powerful beat, and Wil had used it to emphasise the drama.

'As you know, every dance tells a story,' Wil reminded Sienna and Steaphan. 'You must bring that story to life for the few minutes you're performing. Find your characters and show the audience what you're feeling.' He rewound the music. 'Try it again.'

Sienna and Steaphan upped their performance, urged on by Wil.

'Excellent,' Wil told them when they'd finished the piece. 'Now let's try the next part of the routine.

Nothing is finalised yet. I want to see how you tackle the moves, then I'll adjust the choreography to highlight your strengths. I need to see your partnership. So far, I think your styles are well–matched, but you have to develop your rapport.'

'They do look good together though, don't they?' Gareth said to Wil.

'Yes,' Wil confirmed. 'And that's with little rehearsal time together. This means they can elevate their partnership a lot more.'

'To a level where they could win the competition?' said Gareth.

Wil nodded firmly.

Sienna smiled over at Gareth and then at Steaphan. 'We'll put in the work that's necessary.'

Steaphan adjusted his stance as he took Sienna in hold. He nodded and smiled that he was prepared to work hard too.

Delphie enjoyed watching Wil coordinate the routine. Sometimes, she'd try to anticipate the next part of the choreography, but Wil continued to surprise her with his talent for creating a great performance.

At one point, Wil wanted to show Sienna how to improve part of the routine, and beckoned Delphie over to help him demonstrate.

'Watch how we turn and then pause before changing direction and picking up pace with a fast, light moves across the floor,' Wil said to Sienna.

Delphie had seen Sienna try this a few times, and it was always easier to watch someone else dance the routine and then alter it. Delphie knew what was lacking from Sienna, and did her best to show what Wil wanted.

'I get it now,' Sienna said after seeing them dance. She then tried the steps again with Steaphan.

'That's it!' Wil told her. 'I knew you could do it.'

'This should impress the judges at the contest,' Gareth remarked.

'It feels energetic, but I love the control in the choreography,' Steaphan added.

For the remainder of the afternoon, they all helped plan and practise the routine. Delphie partnered with Wil to demonstrate the moves, and gave them a glimpse of a waltz. She enjoyed the whole process.

Wil finally ended the lesson.

'That's enough for today,' Wil announced, switching the music off. 'I'll give you a copy of the footage I've filmed so you can go over it.'

'Can we schedule another session for tomorrow afternoon?' said Gareth.

'Yes, same time,' Wil confirmed.

Sienna and Steaphan, deep in conversation about the routine, headed out. The hotel was a short walk along the main street, and they left Gareth to talk to Delphie and Wil.

'I'm sensing the beginnings of a strong partnership between those two,' Gareth remarked. 'I wasn't sure if Steaphan was right for Sienna, but now...'

'You can never tell until you see them performing,' said Wil. 'A perfect match in theory seldom works. There has to be that spark that they ignite in each other. And that's either there or it's not.'

Gareth nodded, wishing he'd tried harder to keep that spark alight with Delphie.

'Can I talk to you about your artwork?' Gareth said to Delphie.

'Yes, I've been thinking about ideas for the poster,' she said.

She picked up her bag and was getting ready to leave.

Wil was hoping to persuade her to stay and practise some moves, but now Gareth was escorting her out.

Wil walked with them through to the reception.

'I've almost finished the quickstep watercolour for you,' Delphie said to Wil while continuing to leave with Gareth. 'I'll drop it off at the art shop for Callum to frame.'

'I'd be happy to pick it up from you if it's more convenient,' Wil suggested.

'No, it's okay,' said Delphie. 'I'll be in the main street to stock up on fresh groceries anyway.'

She genuinely thought she was being helpful, but Wil smiled tightly, wishing he'd spoken up before Gareth whisked her away.

'I was painting in the barn today, but I've been sketching more ideas for the poster and the show,' Delphie said, chatting happily to Gareth as they walked out of the studio.

Wil watched them go, overhearing them talking as they headed away to her car. An amber glow shone across the street as the day drew to a close.

'I'd love to see this art studio you've set up in the farmhouse barn,' Gareth said, hinting that he wanted to be invited along.

'You're welcome to come up and see it,' said Delphie.

Wil watched Gareth get into Delphie's car. He shook his head in dismay and mentally kicked himself for not asking her to stay and dance at the studio with him.

CHAPTER NINE

'This is a pretty small town,' Gareth remarked, admiring the scenery as Delphie drove them along the country road to the farmhouse. 'But I don't see you settling down here. You're like me. We thrive in the city.'

She explained about looking after her grandparent's property, and that her intention was to go back to Edinburgh.

Gareth nodded as the sunlight flickered through the branches of the trees, and the road cut through the lush landscape. 'If I'd known that you were stepping back into your dancing, I'd have tried to partner you with someone in the city. But I thought you'd put dance aside to forge a career in graphic design and art.'

'I had, and art is first and foremost my aim. Helping Wil with the dancing only came about because he bought one of my paintings and wanted more for his studio. Then he found out I could dance.'

Gareth nodded thoughtfully.

'That's Wil's house over there,' she said as they drove past it.

'Nice house.'

'And the farmhouse is up here,' she added, driving further along the road.

'You're neighbours. That's handy.'

Delphie threw him a glance. 'I told you. I'm not romantically involved with Wil. I'm concentrating on my art.'

Gareth made no further comments or insinuations, and admired the farmhouse as they drove up and parked.

They stepped out into the fresh, country air.

'This is a beautiful farmhouse,' said Gareth. It was far more picturesque than he'd imagined.

'The barn is over here.' Delphie led the way and opened the door wide. She flicked the lights on, illuminating the barn with the twinkle lights and the lamps on her artwork table.

Gareth nodded as he walked in, clearly impressed. 'Now this is what I call an art studio. I can see why you're so productive and spend a lot of time here.'

She waited on him commenting about the dance floor. The canvas sheet only covered her artwork area. But Gareth's attention was on the paintings and the whole art set up.

He saw the drawings she'd been working on for the stage show and picked up her sketch pad.

'I was going to show you the roughs for the stage designs before I started adding details and colours.'

Gareth flipped through the drawings, nodding enthusiastically. 'These are fantastic. I can feel the sense of the winter snow. I love the theatrical atmosphere.'

'If you're okay with these designs, I'll start adding colours.'

'Do that. Send me copies so I can let the show's organisers and director have a look at them.'

'Okay,' said Delphie.

Gareth then admired the paintings on her easels, depicting dancing couples. 'These are magnificent. Do you think you'll have your own studio when you go back to Edinburgh?'

'I don't know. I'm just concentrating on the paintings.'

He wandered around, studying her artwork, and they discussed ideas for the show.

Gareth checked the time. 'I'd better get back to the hotel. I've some calls to make. But thanks for the tour.'

'I'll drive you back down,' she said, switching the lights off in the barn and heading out to the car.

It was a short drive to the main street, and Gareth still hadn't mentioned the barn's dance floor, so Delphie didn't bring it up in their conversation.

She dropped Gareth off outside the hotel, and then drove past the dance studio. On impulse, she decided to pop in to see Wil before going home.

Music sounded from inside as she walked through the reception. Piano playing. She peeked in and saw that Wil was talking to someone on a video call on his laptop.

She hesitated, not wanting to interrupt, but overheard part of their conversation as the piano music stopped.

'Remember,' Wil said to the man, 'don't tell anyone about this.'

'I won't,' the man confirmed.

Delphie went to leave unseen, but Wil caught a glimpse of her.

'Wait, Delphie!'

'I didn't mean to intrude. I was driving by and thought I'd come in for a few minutes.' She heard herself babbling, feeling she'd heard something she wasn't supposed to.

Wil closed the laptop. 'Come in. I was just finishing up for the day.'

He was up to something, and trying to hide it. She was sure of it.

'I was dropping Gareth off at the hotel,' she explained. 'He wanted to see my studio in the barn.'

'I bet he was impressed.'

'He was.' Then she frowned. 'But he never noticed the dance floor.'

'It was one of the first things I noticed in the barn,' said Wil.

'I guess you and Gareth have different views of the world,' she surmised.

'I think we do,' he confirmed. Except when it came to Delphie. They both liked her.

'Well, I'd better be heading home now,' she said.

'Are you working this evening?'

'I'm planning to make some more progress with the show's artwork. Why?'

'I was wondering when you'll give me my next painting lesson.'

'Come along this evening if you want.'

'I'll drop by after dinner,' he said brightly.

'See you then.' Delphie smiled and headed out.

As she drove home, she rewound what she'd overheard at the studio. Obviously, Wil's work involved chatting to lots of dancers about their choreography. But there was a sense of secrecy about the call she'd heard.

She didn't plan to pry, but hoped he'd tell her later.

Wil made himself an easy dinner of a bowl of Scotch broth and bread.

He sat in the kitchen eating his broth and wondering if he should tell Delphie what he was planning.

Undecided, he then showered and changed into his clean, but paint stained top, ready for his art lesson.

A welcoming glow shone from the barn as he drove up and parked.

Delphie was already working on her paintings, but she'd set up an acrylic canvas on an easel for Wil.

'There's an apron for you on the back of your chair,' she said as he walked in.

Wil tied the apron on.

'I've drawn a dancing couple on a canvas. Just a sketch,' Delphie explained. 'And prepared a palette with acrylic paint.'

'Ah, so it's acrylics tonight instead of watercolours. I'm up for that.'

'I've arranged your palette with warm tones, cool tones and neutrals to help you learn how to use them to add interest and contrast to your painting.'

She handed him a couple of brushes. 'Try these brushes. Use the finer one for smaller details. There are other sizes of brushes if you prefer. See what suits you.'

Wil looked at the paints on the palette, wondering how to mix and use them.

Delphie instructed him, showing him the basic techniques and then let him get started.

'Just have a go,' she encouraged him. 'Blend the background with neutral tones. It'll let you get used to how the paint feels on the canvas. Then paint the figures.'

'I like the smooth, thick texture of the acrylics.'

'You can add a wee bit of water if you want, and remember to keep rinsing your brushes in the jars of clean water so you don't muddy the paint on your palette.'

She continued to work on her painting.

'I think I'm better with the acrylics than the watercolours,' he said.

'Yes, you seem to have taken to them well.'

They chatted while they painted, about dancing and art, but Wil didn't reveal his secret.

And Delphie didn't ask.

After Wil painted most of the background, he was keen to paint the figures.

'The photo album is open at the picture that I based the design on,' said Delphie.

Wil put his brush down, cleaned his hands, and had a look at the album that was on one of the tables.

'My grandparents were dancing in the barn. It was a party night years ago.'

Wil studied the photo. 'The barn looks great all done up for the party. You really should think of holding a dance night here.'

Delphie wasn't so quick to dismiss the idea this time. 'Maybe. But it would take quite a bit of organising.'

'I'd help, if you decide to do it before you go back to Edinburgh,' he offered.

And there was that reminder again, the drawing to a close of her stay at the farmhouse even though there was still plenty of time left to enjoy being there.

'I'll think about it,' she said, and then instructed him on painting the figures. 'Use the darker colours on them first, and start to add details with the mid range choices on your palette, then add the highlights.'

Wil tried to follow her advice.

'Use the photo as a guide for the highlights and shadows,' she added.

He noticed the sketches she'd done for the show when he went over to get more white from the tubes of acrylic paint. 'Are these your designs for the show?'

'Some of them. I wanted to make a start on the artwork.'

'That was fast,' said Wil.

Delphie shrugged. 'You know what I'm like.'

He did.

'I haven't forgotten your paintings, or the one for the bakery shop. I just had ideas for the show and wanted to sketch them for Gareth's approval.'

'Multitasking has its merits,' he conceded.

She sighed resignedly. 'Sometimes. But I don't want to paint myself into the same type of corner I was in when I worked in graphic design. I'd no time for anything else.' She glanced at the sketches. 'Though I do love to create new pieces of art, so it doesn't really feel like hard work.'

'I find myself tempted to add more tasks to my schedule,' he said, almost revealing what he was secretly up to. But he buttoned his lips and concentrated again on his painting.

After a while, they both finished painting, and Wil helped her clean up the brushes and the palettes.

'How did I score this evening?' he said. 'Is there a third lesson on offer?'

'There is.' She studied his painting on the easel. 'You've done well with the acrylics. We'll try another round with those.'

'Nothing I paint is ever going to see the light of day hanging up in my studio,' he said. 'But I'd like to keep this acrylic painting as a memento.'

'We'll let it dry on the easel and you can pick it up another night.'

Wil liked that his lessons and time with Delphie weren't finished. While she put the tubes of paint away tidily where she stored them in an old–fashioned dresser, he took his apron off and wandered over to the bar area.

'If you decided to hold a party night in the barn, I'm sure Catriona and Kian could provide the catering and drinks for the bar.'

'I suppose they could,' she agreed, thinking this was a good idea. 'Then all we'd need is the music.'

Wil pressed a button on a control panel behind the bar. The sound system kicked into gear, playing a song they both knew.

Wil bowed playfully. 'Would you care to dance?'

Delphie laughed and played along, placing her hand in his and allowing him to lead her on to the dance floor. The canvas sheeting covered a sliver of the floor, so they were soon waltzing around under the twinkle lights.

Every time Wil held her in his arms, she felt her heart react in ways that could lead her into trouble. But tonight she thought it was worth it, and waltzed with him until the music stopped.

They finished in a close hold, and again he fought the urge to kiss her, but stepped back.

She sensed the underlying feelings between them and a blush rose across her cheeks.

'We'd need a poster to advertise the party night locally,' said Wil, forcing all his attention back to the makeshift plans.

'I wonder where we'll find a graphic designer to make it?' she said.

Wil smiled. 'Callum could print a few copies of whatever you design and we could pin them up in the local shops and the new community hall.'

Suddenly, it seemed feasible to have a dance party at the barn. Delphie smiled brightly. 'Local gossip would soon spread the news too.'

'It could be a popular night.'

Delphie switched the lamps off and glanced around at the barn aglow with twinkle lights. 'Yes, it could.' She went over to the bar and pulled out a large biscuit tin. 'These are tickets from previous parties. The ticket sales cover the basic costs.'

'Can I take one of these with me?'

'Yes.'

'I'd like to talk to Catriona and Kian in the morning, to see if they could handle the catering and the bar,' said Wil.

'Okay.'

As he was leaving, Wil noticed the quickstep watercolour painting. 'This is gorgeous. Do you want me to take it to the art shop for framing?'

Delphie had secured the watercolour to a light board to keep it flat. 'Yes, I'll put a sheet of tracing paper over it for protection.'

Wil carried it carefully to his car and got ready to drive home. 'Thanks again for the art lesson. And the painting. Send me your details. I want to buy all the paintings you've done for me.'

She nodded, and breathed in the night air as she waved him off. A sense of autumn wafted in the breeze, and she hurried over to the farmhouse to make a hot cup of tea.

Wil drove home, leaving the painting safely in the car ready to take to the art shop in the morning.

In his bedroom, he took off his top and got ready for bed. And he thought about Delphie, and the fun he'd had again in her company. Shaking away his feelings, he tried to get some sleep.

Tiredness kicked in after the hectic events of the day and the evening, and he fell sound asleep and didn't stir until the dawn.

Delphie was in night owl mode, sitting up in bed, sketching by the glow of her bedside lamp. She'd lots of ideas for the show, and drew outlines that she planned to work on in the morning.

And she thought about Wil...dancing with him again in the barn. Her grandmother had called earlier to enthuse about the tango video. Now she'd enjoyed another night in Wil's company, culminating in waltzing with him.

Forcing herself to put aside the sketch pad and pencil, she turned the lamp off and settled down, snuggling under the quilt and gazing out at the night sky.

She rewound what Gareth had said... '*I don't see you settling down here. You're like me. We thrive in the city.*'

But here she was living in a large, rambling farmhouse that had plenty of extra rooms, including her bedroom, that she was welcome to stay in. Her grandparents often told her she could stay with them for as long as she wanted. But she'd never taken them up on their offer.

Fluffing her pillows, she tried to settle down. She still tended to agree with Gareth, but she knew she'd miss living at the farmhouse, and she'd miss Wil.

The main street was blinking awake as Wil carried the painting along to the art shop. Callum was open for business and was happy to frame the watercolour to match the others in the dance studio.

'I heard that you and Delphie were swimming in the sea,' Callum remarked. 'And then dancing at the ceilidh.'

'No secrets in this wee town,' said Wil.

'Nope. Everyone knows everyone's business. But that's what I like about living here. Folk help each other. Gossip is handy. Mind you, city types are always secretive. But we soon find out what they're up to.'

Callum meant well, but his comment jarred Wil.

'Oh, you're looking like a man with mischief on his mind,' Callum joked lightly.

'Just a lot on my mind.'

'I'll phone you when the painting is ready to be collected,' Callum said chirpily.

'Thanks, Callum.'

Wil headed out and walked along to the bakery shop that was already busy with customers sitting at the tables having breakfast.

'Are you in for breakfast, Wil?' Kian said to him with a cheery smile.

'Eh, no, but...maybe...' The aroma of fresh cooked Scottish pancakes made him wish he hadn't skipped breakfast.

'It sounds like you're needing a cup of tea and something to eat,' Kian advised. 'Sit down and I'll rustle up a tasty breakfast for you.'

Easily persuaded, Wil sat down and allowed Kian to serve up a mug of tea and a plate of pancakes.

'They're hot off the girdle,' said Kian. 'Help yourself to butter and jam.'

'Thanks, these look delicious.'

'Was there something else you wanted, Wil?'

'Yes, I wanted to talk to you about catering for a party night at Delphie's barn.'

Kian's eyes lit up with interest. 'Are you having a dance night, like her grandparents hold?'

'We're thinking about it.'

'It would save a lot of folk in town from wondering what to do for the annual celebration night.'

Wil tucked into his breakfast and frowned up at Kian.

'Did you not know? Every year, the town has a party to celebrate the start of the autumn. Usually Delphie's grandparents hold a special dance night at the barn. I've heard customers talking about it not being on this year because they're away.'

Catriona overheard their conversation as she went by with a plate of hot buttered toast. 'Is there going to be a party night at the barn?' She sounded hopeful.

'Yes, Wil and Delphie are organising it,' Kian announced, delighted.

'Oh, that's great. People have been wondering where to have the celebration this year. The hotel function rooms are booked for a wedding and an anniversary on the Saturday night, and the community hall is booked solid too,' said Catriona.

'Wil wants us to deal with the catering,' Kian told his wife.

'We'd be glad to do that.' Catriona grinned at Wil. 'We'll plan a buffet and stock up the drinks for the bar.'

Wil ate his breakfast while Kian and Catriona stood beside his table organising everything.

'Delphie's grandparents have a stack of napkins, glasses, plates and cutlery behind the bar,' Kian reminded his wife.

'Remember the big jugs filled with whisky cocktail?' said Catriona.

'That was strong stuff. We'll make sure that's on the drinks menu,' Kian told her.

Catriona hurried away to serve up the toast to a customer.

Kian took out his phone and started to scroll through it. 'I'll check the exact date for the party. Yes, here we are.' He held up his phone to show Wil the Saturday night it should be held.

Wil had a mouthful of buttered pancake and nodded that he agreed with the date.

'Okay, I'll start planning the food and drinks menu,' said Kian, sounding in full efficiency mode. 'I can't wait to let people know there's going to be a party at the barn after all.'

And off he went to start spreading the gossip.

Wil took a sip of his tea and phoned Delphie. 'The party night is on.'

'Did you persuade Kian and Catriona to help with the catering?' said Delphie.

'Apparently, we've solved a problem for the town...' Wil explained the details.

Delphie laughed. 'So we're really going to do this?'

'Oh, yes.'

'You're a bad influence on me,' Delphie said jokingly.

'A party and dancing at the barn, organised by a bad influence and a troublemaker. It sounds like a fun night to me.'

CHAPTER TEN

Wil supped the second mug of tea that Kian served up and gazed out the window. In the background, he listened to the gossip buzzing around the bakery shop.

Kian was on the phone. 'The party night is on at the barn!' Kian told the owner of one of the local hotels. 'We'll need the big barrels of beer delivered there.'

Smiling to himself, Wil sat in the middle of the whirlwind.

Wil's phone rang. It was Callum.

'Do you want me to print the tickets for the party night?' Callum said, sounding eager to take on the task. 'I heard that you and Delphie are organising it after all. I usually print the tickets. I have the date, and it always starts at seven o'clock.'

'Yes, do that, Callum,' Wil agreed.

'Right, I'm on it.' And Callum was gone.

Finishing his tea, Wil got up and went over to the counter and paid for his breakfast.

Kian was still on the phone. Bottles of whisky were being discussed.

'Are the tickets available?' a customer sitting at a table called across to Catriona.

A moment's lull descended over the chatter and all eyes were on Wil.

'Callum is printing them as we speak,' Wil assured them.

The buzz erupted again with customers wanting to put their name down on a list that Catriona was making.

'I'll take two tickets,' a customer called over.

'Put my name down too, Catriona,' another customer added.

Kian finished his call. 'Do you want us to handle the ticket sales?' he said to Wil. 'It would help us gauge how many people need catered for.'

This made sense. 'That would be helpful,' Wil agreed.

A woman, the owner of the local dress shop, hurried in. 'I heard the news. Is there a poster I can put in my shop window?'

'Delphie's designing one,' said Wil.

'What is this year's theme?' the woman wanted to know.

Wil drew a blank.

'Last year the theme was vintage,' Catriona told Wil.

'And the year before that everyone wore kilts and tartan,' the woman added. 'We've had all sorts of themes.'

Wil needed to come up with something fast. 'Dancing,' he said.

'Oh, that's a wonderful theme,' Catriona said, smiling. 'I definitely want a new dress for the party.' She looked at the dress shop owner. 'I'll pop in for a browse of your rails this afternoon.'

The enthusiasm spread around the bakery shop as customers planned what to wear.

Ball gowns and tango dresses were being discussed as Wil's phone rang. It was Callum again.

'What's the party's theme this year?' said Callum.

'Dancing,' Wil told him.

'I'll add that to the information on the tickets. Great theme. Easy for folk to find something to wear. I'll be sure to wear my smart suit.' And Callum was gone again.

Wil finally managed to escape from the melee of the bakery shop. Breathing in the calm morning air, he walked along to his dance studio.

Delphie was in the barn.

She checked the biscuit tin behind the bar. There were the leaflets advertising the party nights from previous years. She planned to use those to create a poster design with the usual information that people needed.

Sitting at her artwork table, she sketched a rough outline, inked it like an illustration, scanned it into her laptop, and added the necessary wording. That's when she noticed that the previous year's poster included a theme. She'd been to dance nights in the barn before, though not in the last few years, but she never knew there was a special party to celebrate autumn.

She phoned Wil. 'We're going to need a theme for the party night.'

'Dancing.' He explained the situation.

'A perfect theme. I'll include it on the poster.' After agreeing this with Wil, she emailed the finished design to Callum at the art shop.

Callum called to confirm he'd received it, and that he'd print out enough copies to distribute locally.

Later in the day, Callum phoned Wil to tell him the watercolour painting was framed ready for collection, and so were the tickets and the posters.

Wil went along to the art shop to pick everything up, and on the way back to the studio he handed in a copy of the poster to the dress shop and to other businesses. Callum had pinned one up in the window of the art shop.

Wil kept a poster for the dance studio, and gave the rest to Catriona and Kian at the bakery shop along with the tickets.

Heading to the dance studio, Wil felt he'd been swept up in the whirlwind of organising the party, and was glad to get back to work on his choreography.

Delphie had gone down to the main street to buy fresh groceries and got caught up in the party buzz circulating the town.

Carrying her shopping back to her car, she thought she'd pop in to see Wil. But as she loaded the groceries into the boot, she noticed Sienna and Steaphan heading into the studio and decided not to interrupt their dance practise.

Back at the farmhouse, Delphie made a cup of tea and took it over to the barn.

Setting up her paints, she made progress with the painting for the bakery shop.

As the afternoon light faded to an evening glow, she received a call from her grandparents. Their cheery faces smiled out at her from the laptop.

'I've so many things to tell you,' Delphie said after hearing that they were still having a great time in Paris. She finally got to the part about the party night. 'I didn't know there was a special party in the barn each year to celebrate autumn.'

'It's always been popular,' said her grandmother.

'We felt we were letting people down this year because we were away on holiday,' her grandfather said, joining in.

'You should've told me,' said Delphie.

'We didn't want to foist that burden on to you,' her grandfather explained. 'We planned to make it up to the town when we got home.'

'It's wonderful that you're holding it this year,' said her grandmother. 'I wish we could be there, but obviously we can't. Though I'm sure it'll be fun with you and Wil hosting it.'

Delphie chatted to her grandparents, and noted information about the running order of the event, from the opening dance to the closing number at the end of the evening.

'You and Wil will need to start the evening with a dance,' her grandmother told her.

'Just the two of us?' Delphie was taken aback.

'Yes,' said her grandmother. 'We always start with a lively number to get the party going. Then we finish with a slow dance, like a romantic waltz.'

'With you and Wil being such fine dancers, it'll be a skoosh for you to do this,' her grandfather added.

'Remember to borrow any dress you want from my wardrobes,' her grandmother reminded her.

After the call, Delphie's mind was whirring with ideas for the dances as she continued to work on the bakery shop painting. Adding pops of colour, like strawberry pink to the cupcakes and bright red to the glacé cherries on top, the painting started to look like an artistic impression of the bakery.

The yellow of the lemon meringue pie, and sugared slices of fruit on top of a lemon drizzle cake, contrasted with the blueberries on the muffins and orange fondant on the carrot cake.

A colourful jar of sweets sat on the counter, and everything from the fresh raspberries on a Victoria sponge, to the Scottish snowball cakes, showed the delicious selection of treats in the bakery shop.

The shop was a joy to paint, and by the time Delphie had finished adding Catriona and Kian into the scene, it was now dark outside and way past dinner.

Leaving the painting to dry, Delphie walked over to the farmhouse kitchen and started to prepare dinner. She'd bought a cottage pie topped with mashed potato at the grocery shop and popped it in the oven to heat while she cut a slice of crusty bread and made a pot of tea.

She was about to serve it up and sit down at the kitchen table when there was a knock on the front door.

Opening it, she found Wil standing there. 'I brought you a copy of the poster and a ticket. I thought you'd like to see them. And I wondered if I could talk to you about the party.'

'I was just about to have dinner.'

'Sorry, I thought you'd have finished it by now.'

'I got caught up in my painting. But would you like to join me? Have you had dinner?'

'No, it's been one of those days, but I don't want to intrude.'

'Come in,' she beckoned, leading him through to the kitchen.

Wil washed his hands at the sink and sat down as she served up two portions of the pie and cut more bread for them.

'How did the choreography practise go with Sienna and Steaphan today?' she said.

Wil blinked.

'I saw them going into the studio when I was picking up my groceries,' she explained. 'I was planning to pop in to see you, but I didn't want to interrupt their rehearsal.'

'It went well. You should've come in.'

Delphie poured their tea. 'I spoke to my grandparents about the party night. We're supposed to open with a dance.'

Wil cut–in. 'I know. People are expecting a proper performance from us. And a closing number.'

'I thought it was just to encourage everyone on to the dance floor.'

Wil shook his head. 'Not for us. Rumours are circulating that we're putting on two full performances.'

Delphie tried not to smile and ate a mouthful of mashed potatoes and gravy.

'What's so funny?' he said, starting to smile too.

She took a sip of tea. 'I thought I was busy in the city, but for a quiet small town, it's buzzing. The days are whizzing by.'

Wil agreed. 'But I'm enjoying myself more than I have in a long time.'

'So am I.'

They both burst out laughing.

'Okay, what will we do for our opening number?' said Wil.

'My gran says they always dance something lively. How about a quickstep?'

'Or I could twirl you around during a swing dance,' he joked, gesturing that he'd hold her above his head and spin her like a baton. 'That would liven things up.'

The look she gave him vetoed his idea.

'A quickstep would be ideal,' he agreed.

'Or you could perform a solo ballet number,' she teased him. 'Leaping high into the air and doing pirouettes across the floor.'

'My ballet tights will be in the wash that day.'

'Ah, well, maybe another time.'

They continued to tease each other and enjoy their dinner.

'Mind if I have a look at the dance floor in the barn?' he said as he finished helping her wash and dry the dinner dishes. 'I'd like to have a proper look at the size of it if we're going to perform.'

'Yes, come on over.' Delphie led the way, shivering slightly in the night air after the cosiness of the kitchen. But once she was inside the barn, the warmth wrapped itself around her.

Wil started to scope out the floor. 'It's quite large so we should be able to quickstep across the diagonals at speed easily.'

Delphie looked around. 'The barn can hold a fair number of people. It's going to be jumping at the party. I'll obviously move my artwork into the farmhouse out of the way and that'll make even more room for dancing.'

Wil clasped her hand. 'Try a quickstep with me. See how it feels.'

They fell into step with each other and danced across the floor.

'This could work,' she said, sensing that spark whenever she was dancing with Wil. 'But we should try it with music.'

'I'll check what's on the song list at the bar later, but for the moment, let's dance to this.' Wil scrolled through his phone and found a piece of lively music.

As the song played, Wil led Delphie in a quickstep. They danced until the song ended, smiling as they skip–stepped together around the floor.

'Let's try a different song,' Wil suggested, and lined up another song on his phone. 'Round two,' he said playfully.

Delphie played along, enjoying having fun with Wil.

She could feel the strength in the muscles beneath his shirt contrasting with his lightness of movement when they skip–stepped to the beat. He was the best dancer she'd ever been partnered with.

When the song finished they both assessed the music.

'The first song suited us better,' he concluded.

'It did.' She shrugged. 'Round three?' she said, and suggested another song.

'Great choice. I hadn't thought about that one.' Wil set the song to play and took her in hold.

The introduction to the song was longer than the others and allowed them to have a moment standing there, smiling at each other, waiting for the beat to kick in.

Delphie felt her heart was pounding with the excitement of being so close to Wil rather than the dance.

In sync, they both began dancing the quickstep, poised, in perfect hold.

It was one of those times that Delphie knew she'd always remember. Their impromptu quickstep that night in the barn. And for a moment, just a heartbeat, she pictured what her life would be like if she was together with Wil. Dating him. A true romance. Something that had eluded her despite her best efforts to find the perfect partner.

After they finished, they both agreed that the first song was the winner. The introduction was lively at the start and suited the quickstep better.

'The first song would be my choice,' said Wil.

'Mine too.'

She'd taken her hand off his shoulder, and he'd released his hand from her waist, but they were both clasping one hand as they stood there discussing the music.

And then he let her go, stepped back and picked up his phone where he'd sat it down on the edge of her artwork table.

'I should go and not take up any more of your time,' he said. 'We'll rehearse the quickstep another evening.'

'We could continue to practise now if you want. Though I'd like to run over to the farmhouse and put on my dancing shoes.'

A smile lit up Wil's face. 'Great, I'll set up the music again.'

'Could you move my artwork table to the side so that we can use the entire floor?'

More than willing to do this, he began to set things up.

Delphie hurried out into the night, and ran upstairs to her room. She was wearing a skirt and top that were fine for dancing, but she put on a pair of dance shoes with heels, then hurried back over to the barn.

Wil had carefully moved her artwork table and easels aside, clearing the floor.

And all of a sudden, Delphie saw the barn as a dance venue rather than her temporary art studio. Images from the past flickered through her mind, remembering the times she'd been there years ago when her grandparents hosted a party night.

Wil stood in the middle of the floor and gestured around. 'It really is quite spacious.'

'It is. Even when there's live entertainment on stage, or the bar is busy, the dance floor dominates the barn. My grandfather designed it with this in mind so that my grandmother had a spacious floor to dance on.'

'How to you feel about elevating the quickstep routine?' said Wil.

'I'm ready to up my game.'

A warmth touched Wil's heart. He loved that Delphie was willing to give things a go.

He walked over to her and she gazed up at him, into those blue eyes that reminded her so much of her favourite cerulean when painting.

'If we're going to use the song we've selected, we can add to the drama on the intro beats,' he said. 'We'll begin in promenade, and then do a flick step into the dance, adding a bit of flair from the start.'

Wil demonstrated on his own, showing Delphie what he had in mind.

She tried it, jump stepping into the movement.

'That's it!' he said. 'Then we'll spring–step across the diagonal.' Again he danced on his own, ending up at the far corner of the floor. 'We'll add a sway, and then with another flick step, kick out the back foot, before circling the floor for one complete loop. If that makes sense.'

'Total sense.'

Wil smiled, eager to try this. He liked that she picked up on his moves easily from her background in dance. But it was more than that. It felt like they were on the same wavelength whenever they danced together. Could they ever be so in tune off the dance floor he wondered. Pushing this thought aside, he turned the music on and took her in hold.

And they danced, adding the flicks and kicks.

He stopped and paused the music halfway through. 'Now let's add some extra moves at the midway point where we cross in front and cross behind.'

Every move Wil suggested, Delphie went along with, enjoying being part of the choreography.

As they practised each part of the dance, she felt them tap in time, lock step in line and chassé in sync.

'Okay,' he said, 'let's try the whole dance again — with pizzazz.'

Delphie laughed. 'Pizzazz coming up.'

Wil paused. 'It's a pity we won't have this on film.'

'Hang on.' She set–up the camera on her laptop.

Wil posed in different areas of the floor while she altered the camera angle to capture everything.

She laughed as he included a few playfully exaggerated poses, loving the fun they were having while making sure they had a routine that people would enjoy watching.

'Lights!' Wil announced.

Delphie turned her desk lamp off to create a sparkling atmosphere with the twinkle lights.

'Camera!' he said.

Delphie gave him the thumbs up. 'We're good to go.'

'Action!' Wil pulled Delphie into his arms as the music started, and they were off to a flying start.

Delphie danced with all the pizzazz he'd hoped for, and they matched each other so well that when they finished, they were both breathless and smiling from the fun of it.

'That was wonderful, Delphie,' Wil murmured, gazing at her, so close, again a breath away from her lips.

They both sensed where their feelings could lead them and stepped back. Wil bowed and Delphie curtsied to conclude the performance.

Delphie went over to the laptop that was set up on her artwork table at the side of the dance floor. She checked the recording and smiled.

Every moment of the dance was captured on film. Wil stood beside her as she played the video. They nodded throughout the performance, agreeing that they'd nailed the routine they'd use as the opening number. But then his heart ached, as he saw the romantic moment at the end of the dance.

'You're an excellent performer,' he said, clearing his throat of emotion. It was too much to hope that they had a future together when their worlds were due to be far apart.

'As are you, Wil.'

He rubbed his hands together. 'Well, I'd better be going. It's late and we've got one routine in the bag.'

'I'll send you a copy of the video,' she said, turning off the twinkle lights in the barn as she saw him out.

In the cold evening air, she closed the barn door on what was a true night to remember, and waved as Wil drove away.

CHAPTER ELEVEN

Bright morning sunlight shone outside the barn as Delphie worked on the designs for Gareth. She phoned him to update him on the artwork.

'I've inked more of the sketches to a finished artwork level,' she told him. 'I'm heading down to the town with a painting for the bakery shop. I thought I'd hand them into you at the hotel.'

'I'm not at the hotel,' Gareth told her.

'Well, wherever you are in town. We can arrange to meet and I'll give you the designs.'

'I'm back in Edinburgh,' Gareth revealed.

Delphie blinked. 'Edinburgh?'

'I drove home last night. I only planned to stay at the hotel for a few days,' he reminded her.

'Yes, but I assumed you'd at least let me know you were leaving.'

'Sorry, my focus has been on working with Sienna and Steaphan, organising other auditions, and I'm busy with the show. But email me the designs. I'm meeting the show's director later today.'

The scenario was familiar. Gareth used to make his own plans, often forgetting to tell her. Not that he was obliged to do this, but it always made her feel like she was on the outskirts of his life rather than at the heart of it.

'I'll do that,' she said, disguising how she felt.

'Thanks, Delphie. I hope you're not annoyed with me because I left without telling you.'

'Not at all,' she lied.

After the call, she took a moment to adjust her senses. This was typical of Gareth, but as she sat in the barn gazing out at the sunlight, breathing in the fresh country air, she realised he'd done her a favour.

Without further hesitation, she emailed the designs to Gareth and then closed her laptop. She still wanted to create the designs for the show, especially as a lot of the artwork was complete. But if Gareth was happy to deal with the work via email, he'd released her from the pressure of having to go back to Edinburgh if she didn't want to. Or at least in her own sweet time.

Wrapping up the acrylic painting for the bakery shop, she put it in the back of her car and drove down to the town. Sunlight flickered through the trees, and she drove with the window open, feeling the pressure cooker of her schedule lift a little.

Parking outside the bakery shop, she carried the painting inside.

Catriona and Kian's faces lit up with anticipation. 'Is that the painting?'

Delphie had wrapped it in light, glassine paper to protect it. 'Yes, it's ready for hanging.'

'Oh, let's see it,' said Catriona.

Customers sitting at the tables paused from enjoying midmorning tea and coffee to view the painting.

Kian helped Delphie hold the painting while she carefully unwrapped it.

'It's wonderful!' Kian announced, holding it up to show Catriona, and then letting the customers see it.

From the delighted look on everyone's faces the painting was going to be a popular addition to the bakery shop.

Kian asked Delphie's advice on how to hang it up properly on the wall behind the front counter, and together they tackled the task.

'There you go,' said Delphie.

'I love it,' Catriona announced, standing back to admire it.

Customers chimed–in with praise for the painting.

Seeing the colours of the painting to full advantage under the lights of the bakery shop, Delphie was pleased that the pastel tones benefited from the pops of bright red, pink, yellow and blue.

Leaving them to enjoy their painting, Delphie walked to her car and saw Sienna and Steaphan coming out of the dance studio, presumably having finished rehearsing with Wil. So she decided to drop by to talk to him.

The studio was quiet when she walked into the reception, but then she heard the piano music like before. The dramatic notes of the music sounded wonderful, and she ventured in to find Wil dancing a routine she'd never seen before.

Unaware that she was watching him, he took full advantage of the empty dance floor, leaping and spinning as if performing in a classic ballet, though not one she recognised. Then he flowed into a sweeping ballroom routine and only stopped when he saw her reflected in the mirror.

'Delphie!' he gasped, and hurried over to switch the music off, giving the impression that she'd caught him dancing something she wasn't meant to see. That secretive quality she'd sensed from him before.

'I'll go,' she offered immediately, turning to hurry away.

'No, wait,' he beckoned. 'Come in. I was just...' He didn't finish telling her and merely ran his hands through his hair in an awkward manner.

She couldn't fathom out what was wrong. He was the one to always encourage her to pop in to see him.

'If you're working on choreography for Sienna and Steaphan—'

Wil cut–in. 'No, I'm not. It's not for anyone in particular.'

His response puzzled her even more, so she changed the subject. 'Gareth has gone back to Edinburgh.'

Wil walked towards her, those eyes of his full of intensity. 'Sienna mentioned this. She was here with Steaphan. We were adjusting the choreography for their routine.'

Delphie nodded. 'Yes, I saw them leaving. I was handing in Catriona and Kian's painting to the bakery shop. They seem happy with it.'

'I must go along and have a look,' he said.

Delphie sensed that they were sidestepping the issue of what Wil was secretly up to, so when his phone rang, she left him to talk to another dancer about their choreography.

'I'll see myself out.'

She noticed that he'd pinned up a copy of the poster behind the reception.

Outside the dance studio, she took a deep breath, feeling unsettled, and she jolted when her phone rang. It was Gareth.

'I know it's short notice, Delphie,' he began excitedly, 'but I'm having lunch with the show's director tomorrow in Edinburgh, and he wants to meet you. I showed him your latest designs and he's impressed with your ideas and wants to discuss pushing ahead with your artwork. The set designer and others will be there.'

Delphie hesitated. It wasn't too far to drive to Edinburgh, but somehow she'd locked off that part of her world for the time being, enjoying the seclusion of the town.

'Can you join us?' Gareth urged her. He told her the details of the lunch meeting.

Delphie glanced back at the dance studio, and made her decision. 'Yes, I'll be there.'

'Bring any other designs you have with you,' Gareth advised her.

'I'll work on a few more tonight,' she said. 'I've ideas for the show's opening scenery to create a wonderful atmosphere. It would be handy to discuss this with the director and the set designer.'

'Great, I'll see you tomorrow,' he said, sounding delighted.

As Delphie walked along to her car, a message came through from Wil.

Have dinner with me tonight at my house. We'll talk about the choreography you saw me practising.

A double–edged dagger cut through her heart. On one side, she wanted to have dinner with Wil, to see his house, and to talk to him about what he was planning. If only he'd invited her sooner. But she was already committed to going to the city and needed to work on the extra designs. Considering the artwork she wanted to take with her, she'd be busy sketching and painting for the rest of the day and into the evening.

Gareth just phoned. I need to work tonight on my designs for the show. I have a lunch meeting in Edinburgh tomorrow with Gareth, the show's director and others.

Wil muttered under his breath, wishing he'd invited her earlier.

Good luck with your meeting. See you when you get back.

Their messages ended there, but she felt the lingering doubt and regrets between them as she drove back to the farmhouse.

Wil locked the front door of the dance studio and put the piano music on loud, as if to drown out the feelings of frustration. He should've told her the first time about his plans. He'd seen the questioning looks she'd given him. But he wanted to tell her properly, not in a brief conversation. Now, she was having lunch with Gareth in Edinburgh, back in the city where she once belonged.

Standing in front of the mirrors, he began dancing — strong, dramatic opening moves in time to the melodic waves building from the music resonating around him.

But nothing drowned out the feelings he had for Delphie. Or the gnawing doubt that he missed his chance for happiness with her.

Delphie worked in the barn, creating the new designs for the show throughout the rest of the day and into the early evening.

She tried not to think about Wil and put her focus on the artwork. Satisfied she had the designs she needed, she put them carefully into a portfolio ready to take with her to Edinburgh the following day.

Turning off the lights in the barn, she walked over to the farmhouse, noticing that the night sky was overcast with barely any stars to be seen. A storm was brewing. She could feel it in the air, and hurried into the warmth of the kitchen.

While dinner cooked in the oven, she wandered through to one of the rooms where she pictured she'd set up her artwork when the barn was being used for the party night. Her grandmother sometimes used this room for crafting, and the window overlooked the garden.

As the timer pinged on the oven, she went back through to the kitchen and served up the casserole for her dinner. Plans for the things she wanted to discuss at the meeting in Edinburgh flickered through her mind. Gareth had given her a rough idea of what they'd talk about over lunch.

Finishing dinner, she tidied up and decided to have an early night.

Lying in bed, she pulled the quilt up and watched the dark clouds swirling across the night sky. Snuggling under the covers, she tried not to think of any impending storms.

Wil drove home at night from the dance studio after a busy day.

He parked outside his house and walked up the garden path, noticing the angry sky above the countryside. The heady scent of the flowers indicated that rain was due.

If Delphie had accepted his dinner invitation, he'd have made an effort to cook a meal for them, but instead, he made himself a couple of slices of hot buttered toast and a mug of tea.

Wil ate this in the living room, having lit the fire, and sat watching the flames flicker in the hearth...and thought about Delphie's meeting in Edinburgh.

He genuinely hoped it went well for her. But he was concerned that Gareth would sweet talk her into changing the plans she'd made to enjoy her time in the town, away from the hustle and bustle of the city. Now she was heading back to where she once belonged. This could change everything if she was persuaded to step back into her busy life in Edinburgh, perhaps splitting her time between there and the farmhouse.

Drinking down his tea to wash away the bitter taste of regret that he hadn't handled things better, he settled down at the fireside and wrote notes for his choreography while listening to another piece of the piano music in the background.

His large notepad was filled with ideas for creative routines, character notes, rough sketches and plans.

By the time the last embers of the fire burned themselves out, he'd made more progress with this, and put his notes aside.

Turning off the lights, he went to bed.

In the shadowed darkness, he watched the stormy sky, wondering if it was all bluff and thunder, or whether it would rain during the night.

Storm clouds pressed the breath out of the day as Delphie left the farmhouse the next morning and got into her car.

It hadn't rained overnight, but she put her trench coat on the back seat of the car, along with her portfolio, in case it was bucketing down in Edinburgh.

She wore a classy grey skirt suit and white chemise, with two–tone grey court shoes. An outfit from her graphic design days in the office. Smart and stylish. The only colourful aspect about her was the artwork tucked into her portfolio.

Driving off, she headed down the coast, catching glimpses of the sea through the trees and greenery.

From there, she drove over the bridge that spanned the Firth of Forth, and headed towards Edinburgh, into the heart of the city.

The sun was tussling with the grey clouds, trying to fight its way through. Neither was winning. This clash created a dramatic backdrop to the city's magnificent skyline. Historic buildings were silhouetted against the impending storm along with the spires rising up towards the slivers of bright sun.

After parking her car, she put her coat on, and carrying her bag and portfolio, she walked towards the restaurant where she was due to have lunch.

The familiar sights and sense of the city made her feel like she'd been thrown back into her old life, especially as she was due to meet with Gareth. Some things never changed, and yet she felt so different being there. Edinburgh hadn't skipped a beat since she'd left. But she felt out of step with it.

Shrugging off her uneasiness, she walked into the restaurant armed to the teeth for the meeting.

Wil dashed in the rain from the dance studio along to the bakery shop for lunch.

Shaking off the droplets, he sat at a window table, gazing out through the rain, thinking that the scene looked like one of Delphie's watercolours.

Kian handed him a lunch menu. 'We've got a rainy day special. A bowl of lentil soup with wholemeal bread, followed by our tasty stew and dumplings.'

Wil handed back the menu. 'I'll have the special. It sounds delicious.'

'What do you think of our painting?' Kian said, gesturing to it hanging behind the counter. 'Customers are fair taken with it.'

Wil admired the artwork. 'It's great. I love the colours.' He compared it to the selection of cakes on display. 'And you and Catriona are instantly recognisable.'

Kian nodded and smiled. 'We are. We're so pleased with it.' Then he hurried away to get Wil's order.

Wil gazed over at the painting. Delphie's dance figures were beautiful, but she'd really captured Kian and Catriona in their bakery shop. Seeing the painting made him wonder if she was now having lunch in Edinburgh. He glanced through the rain on the window. A mix of emotions unsettled him, from missing her, to hoping that Gareth wasn't trying to inveigle Delphie into a situation that suited him rather than her.

'You're looking a wee bit peely–wally the day,' Kian said to Wil as he served up his soup and bread. 'Dancing yourself into a shadow no doubt. We've seen the lights on late at night in your studio. Careful you don't burn the candle to the wick.'

Wil nodded and smiled at Kian's advice, and then tucked into his hot bowl of soup.

Gareth stood up from the table to greet Delphie as she walked over to join them.

He introduced her to the director and three others, one of them the show's set designer.

Delphie wasn't late. They'd all met up slightly early and had been chatting about the show when she arrived.

Sitting down next to Gareth, she was soon steeped in conversation with the director seated opposite her.

'I see you have your portfolio with you,' said the director. 'Did you bring the new designs?'

'I did. I finished them last night.' She assumed they wouldn't look at them until after lunch, but the director and the others were eager to see her artwork.

Delphie lifted up the portfolio where she'd rested it at the side of her chair, and began to explain each piece to them.

From their reaction, she'd hit the right notes with her designs.

'With these designs, we'll be able to plan the production now,' the director told her.

The set designer nodded. 'Often we're running late trying to get the sets ready for the show. Having all of this coordinated puts us well ahead of schedule.'

'Delphie's background, from working as a graphic designer in Edinburgh, has enabled her to produce finished artwork to tight deadlines,' Gareth said to them.

'I'm impressed with your work, Delphie,' the director told her. 'We're pleased to include you in the show's production.'

A dagger of doubt stabbed through Delphie, and she shot a look at Gareth. What had he promised them?

Gareth caught the look and explained. 'Delphie is currently living in a farmhouse up the coast where she's working on her paintings.'

'We're happy to work around your schedule,' the director assured her. 'Besides, we've got most of what we need right now to make substantial headway with the show.'

The relief showed in Delphie, and she relaxed a little.

Over lunch, they continued to chat about their plans for the show, and the lunch spilled into a long afternoon discussing everything from the poster design to the lighting and costumes. Delphie enjoyed hearing how the whole process of the show was fitted together, and it was only when the daylight outside the window faded that she realised it was almost dinner time.

The lights of Edinburgh glittered like diamonds in the darkness, and the grand structures of the historic buildings were silhouetted against the night sky.

The director and the others bid Delphie and Gareth goodnight and headed out.

Gareth smiled at Delphie. 'That went well.'

'It did.' She picked up her bag and got ready to leave too.

Gareth helped her on with her coat. 'The rain has held off all day, but it looks like it's going to pour down.'

They walked out of the restaurant and paused outside.

Delphie shivered, feeling the cold air had quite a bite to it, and it had started to rain.

'I've been invited to dinner.' Gareth pointed to a hotel and restaurant nearby. 'Come and join us. It's just a few friends, dancers, those involved with the show, the contests.'

The rain became heavier, and she felt the sting of it on her face.

'I should get back to my car and head home,' she said.

'Nonsense, you'll be soaked by the time you get halfway along the road.' Clasping her arm, he ran with her across the road to the hotel, shielding her from the brunt of the rain.

They shook the rain off themselves off in the hotel foyer. He checked in her coat and other items at reception.

'The party's through here,' Gareth said, leading her into the restaurant to meet his friends.

A loud clap of thunder sounded from outside, causing Delphie to jolt.

'It's going to be a wild, stormy night,' Gareth added.

Delphie didn't doubt it. Somehow, she was now about to party with Gareth in a venue they both knew well from their past together in Edinburgh.

Several smiling faces greeted Delphie and Gareth as they joined them. Delphie recognised a couple of the faces, dancers she'd met before in the city.

Everyone was getting ready to order dinner.

Delphie was pulled into the hub of their night.

Screams and laughter erupted when a flash of lightning lit up the window.

Lightning never strikes twice in the same place, Delphie thought to herself, and she had no plans to repeat her past mistakes with Gareth.

CHAPTER TWELVE

Wil was still fired up on the fumes of the stew he'd had for lunch as he danced into the evening at the studio. Another night of burning the candle to the wick.

He'd promised himself he wouldn't repeatedly check his phone for messages from Delphie, and continued to break it as he changed the music to perform another piece of choreography.

He hoped she was okay. The rain had eased off in the town during the day, but she'd still be driving back on a stormy night.

Knowing her character, he doubted she'd be back at the farmhouse without having the courtesy to send him a message that she was home.

There were no windows in the dance area, so he walked through to the reception and looked out the front door. The street glistened with the remnants of the rain that had now stopped, but the sky still bore the storm clouds. No one was out and about at this time of night.

Taking his phone from his pocket he decided to send Delphie a message.

It's been a stormy day, and night. I hope you're okay.

As he pressed send, a message came through for him from Delphie. He blinked. She couldn't have responded instantly. It meant that they'd both messaged each other at the same time.

I'm still in Edinburgh, but I'll be driving home soon.
Thanks for telling me.
I'll let you know when I arrive back.

The relief he felt soothed his heart, and he realised he'd been more anxious than he'd imagined.

Delphie put her phone in her bag, smiling to herself that Wil had contacted her at the same time she'd messaged him.

Gareth was trying to persuade her to stay overnight in Edinburgh as she collected her coat at the hotel reception. The party had been fun, with laughter and dancing. With all of them being capable dancers, they'd enjoyed getting up on the dance floor throughout the evening. Delphie had danced several times with Gareth, and although she caught a glimpse of past times when they'd been happy together, those times were long gone. And now it was time for her to go home too. She'd opted to drink mineral water during the evening so she'd be fit to drive.

'It's not that far to drive home,' Delphie said to Gareth, sidestepping his idea for her to book a room at the hotel for an overnight stay. He hadn't included himself in that suggestion, but she sensed that one word of encouragement from her would've been all that was necessary.

Gareth sighed wearily. 'You're being silly. Stay overnight.'

Delphie stood her ground with a smile. 'No, I want to go home. The roads will be quiet at this time of night.'

Gareth nodded but insisted he drop her off at her car. His was parked nearby.

Taking him up on his sensible offer, she stepped out of his car and got into hers.

'Thanks Gareth,' she said.

'We'll talk soon.'

They then drove off in different directions across Edinburgh.

Delphie's route took her to the bridge across the Firth of Forth, and in what seemed like no time, she was driving back up the coast road to the town.

This was the direction her life was taking. She was even more sure of it than ever. But she still had time to think what she wanted to do before her grandparents came home. Living in the farmhouse felt safe but exciting, and opened up possibilities she'd never ventured to try during her busy life in the city.

Glimpses of the silvery grey sea shimmered in the dark. Not too far now until she was on the country road leading to the small town.

Wil continued dancing for at least another half an hour after Delphie's message, bolstered that she was coming home.

Finally, he turned the lights off in the studio, locked the front door and walked along to where his car was parked. No one else was around, and despite the cold breeze blowing through his open neck white shirt, he felt a warmth in his heart for the wee town.

The overarching trees along the country road shimmered in the darkness, the leaves damp from the recent downpour. Puddles had drained off into the surrounding lush fields, leaving the road easy to navigate.

As he drove towards his house, he noticed car headlights behind him, as another car turned off the main route on to the country road.

Squinting against the glare in the mirrors, he tried to see if it was a farm vehicle, willing to pull aside if it needed to get by him.

Whoever was driving dipped their beams, or they were flashing their lights at him.

Unsure he kept driving, getting closer to his house where he'd be pulling over anyway.

As he drove into his front garden, the car followed close by, and it was only then that he realised it was Delphie.

Wil parked, jumped out of the car and couldn't wait to greet her.

'You're home!' he said.

Delphie pulled up and spoke to him out the window. 'Yes. I assume you've just finished at the studio.'

'I have. It's been a long but productive day. How did your meeting go in Edinburgh?'

'Excellent. It was a worthwhile trip, even though I'm back so late. But the meeting rolled into the late afternoon, and then Gareth invited me to have dinner at a hotel restaurant nearby with a few of his friends. They're dancers, so I ended up dancing too, while waiting for the thunder and lightning storm to ease.'

'It's been a stormy day here as well.'

His words hung in the damp air for a moment, and then he decided to invite her in.

'I'm about to make a cuppa,' he said. 'Would you like to join me? I know it's late, but...' he shrugged.

Delphie got out of the car. 'I'm not watching the clock tonight.'

Neither was Wil.

Seeing her heels dig into the soggy grass, Wil instinctively lifted her up and carried her the few steps to the front door. 'You don't want to ruin your shoes.'

Feeling his strength lift her as if she was lightweight, Delphie's heart pounded, but the cold breeze kept her blush in check.

Placing her down carefully, Wil unlocked the front door, stepped inside and flicked the lights on.

'I'll light the fire,' he said, striding through to the living room where the fire was set ready to light. 'The house will start to heat up soon.' He gestured upstairs. 'My bedroom is up there. Help yourself to a jumper if you want.'

The white chemise beneath the grey jacket of her skirt suit did little to keep her cosy, so while Wil went through to make the tea in the kitchen, she took him up on his offer and went upstairs.

He'd mentioned that he'd leased the house already furnished, so the decor and styling wasn't his. But she could see why he liked living here. The neutral tones of the walls and the large rugs on the polished wooden floor had a classy quality. Left to his own devices, Wil would have decorated the house in a similar style.

She found his bedroom located at the end of the top floor hallway, and ventured in. Turning on a lamp, she noticed that he kept his room tidy. The bed was made, clothes put away, and no mess that she could see without being a fusspot.

Opening the wardrobe doors, she saw the shirts and trousers he wore daily that had a stretch in them suitable for dancing. Shelves down the side of the wardrobe had a selection of folded jumpers and tops. She picked out a soft grey jumper, took her jacket off and put the jumper on over her chemise. It felt instantly cosy, if rather large. She folded the sleeves up.

Taking a brief peek around, including peering out the window at the view across the countryside, she then turned the light off, picked up her jacket and went back down the stairs.

In the quietude of the house, she heard Wil rattling around in the kitchen making the tea and the fire crackling into life in the living room.

She hung her jacket on a peg in the hall, and went over to the fire to warm her hands. A real log fire was something of a novelty. There was no such thing in her flat in Edinburgh. She'd always loved the cosy fires at the farmhouse, but she'd yet to light one. Now that the warmer weather looked like it was calling it a day, she aimed to light one too.

'Would you like something to eat?' Wil called to her.

She went through to join him in the kitchen. 'Tea's fine. I enjoyed a nice lunch, though I did more nattering than munching. And I opted for a light salad and mineral water at the dinner party.'

'I had a rainy day special at the bakery shop. Apart from that, little else except cups of tea. Oh and, Kian and Catriona say that the tickets are selling like hot cakes.'

'I'm glad,' she said, noticing a Dundee cake in the kitchen. The fruit cake was topped with almonds and was one of her favourites.

Wil saw her eyeing the cake. 'I bought this from the bakery shop. Kian says it's a traditional recipe. Would you like a slice with your tea?'

Taking Delphie's smile as her reply, Wil cut two slices and served them on plates.

Carrying the tea tray through to the living room, he put it down on the table in front of the fire.

'Cheers,' he said, holding up his teacup.

Delphie tipped her cup against his. 'Cheers.'

She bit into her cake, enjoying the rich fruit taste. Then she gave him the short course on her meeting in Edinburgh.

'How did it feel to be back in the city?' he said.

'Different, like I used to belong there, but I wanted to be back here.'

Wil took this in. 'Maybe you belong here.'

With a mouthful of cake she nodded.

Wil smiled at her.

She took a sip of tea. 'This is a lovely house,' she commented. 'Parts of the design remind me of the farmhouse. They were probably built around the same era.'

'The kitchens are similar. Nice big kitchens.'

'No wonder you seemed so at home in the farmhouse kitchen.'

'The company had a lot to do with it.'

She blushed, hoping to blame the heat from the fire.

'There's an option to buy the house on the lease,' he revealed.

'Do you think you'll do that?'

'It depends.'

'On whether you find a better life here with your dance studio in the town?' she prompted him.

He shrugged. 'Sienna and Steaphan are leaving tomorrow afternoon after another practise at the studio,' he remembered to tell her. 'They're going back to Edinburgh.'

'Do you think they have a chance of winning the contest?'

He hesitated. 'I did, until today.'

'What happened?'

'They came in to refine their routine,' he explained. 'But Sienna decided to change parts of the choreography.'

Delphie blinked. 'Why? I thought you'd created a great routine for them.'

'Sienna saw clips of another competitor's routine and wants to add even more drama and tricky moves.' From Wil's tone he obviously didn't agree.

'Did you tell Sienna this would be a mistake?'

'She's stubborn. So their routine's now changed. Steaphan is going along with what Sienna wants. But I think it highlights their weaknesses instead of enhancing their strengths.'

'I guess it's up to them, but I think your choreography is wonderful.'

Wil smiled warmly at her as the flickering light from the fire emphasised his handsome face.

A vintage clock chimed a late hour that neither of them wanted to think about.

Delphie stood up and stretched, reluctant to leave the cosiness of sitting in front of the fire with Wil to head out into the cold night. But it was a short drive along the road to the farmhouse, so she kept his jumper on and he escorted her out.

He took her by surprise when he lifted her over the damp grass and placed her down beside her car.

She got in, turned the engine on, and spoke to him out the window. 'Thanks for the tea and chatter.'

'Anytime,' he said, meaning it. 'Would you like to have dinner here with me tomorrow night? I know you've been wondering about the new choreography you've seen me working on, dancing to the classical piano music. I'd like to talk to you about that, but where it's private and we won't be rushed or interrupted.'

He'd made it clear that whatever secret he'd been keeping from her, he wanted to reveal.

'I'll come over around seven,' she said, and then she drove off.

Wil stood in the cold night and waved her off, watching the tail lights of her car disappear into the darkness. Then he went inside and locked the door.

The two minute drive wasn't enough time to heat the car up, and she was grateful for the warmth of Wil's woolly jumper.

Grabbing her things from the back seat, she hurried inside and went upstairs to get ready for bed.

Jumping under the covers for warmth, she felt the tiredness of the long day and longer night hit her hard.

She started to wonder what Wil was up to, but she fell asleep as the sound of the wind swirling over the farmland helped lull her into a deep slumber.

Wil checked the kitchen cupboards and made a list of the groceries he'd need to make dinner for them. Having enjoyed the stew at the bakery shop, he decided to make a similar stew for their dinner.

He liked having tea by the fire with Delphie and was looking forward to having dinner with her.

Securing the fire, he went upstairs to bed, planning all the things he wanted to talk to her about over dinner.

The wind whipped through the trees in the garden, but he liked the cosy seclusion of the house, especially on nights like this.

Wil drove down to the dance studio in the morning, knowing he had a busy day ahead, but his thoughts were on planning dinner. The morning whizzed by in a blur of phone calls, talking to dancers about their choreography and viewing videos of their routines.

The morning was brighter but blustery, so Delphie kept the barn door closed while she worked on her latest painting, beginning with a sketch, and then drawing it on to the canvas.

Setting up her acrylic paints on her palette, she began to paint the vast night sky, sprinkled with stars, arching above the farmhouse. Wil had suggested she paint a couple dancing under the stars, and as she'd caught up on most of her artwork, she decided to attempt it.

On the way to the barn she'd taken a photo of the farmhouse so she could draw it to scale. And on her laptop she'd paused the video of the quickstep she'd danced recently with Wil. There they were, dancing in perfect harmony, poised, in hold, and she'd sketched them into the painting in front of the farmhouse.

The figures were in the foreground, with the dramatic sky arching over them.

Mixing ultramarine on her palette, she painted the sky, adding Prussian blue to create depth and interest.

Raw and burnt umber emphasised the structure of the farmhouse and blended well with the blue tones.

The stars were mainly bright titanium white, some with a touch of yellow to make it look as if the stars were twinkling. At least, that was the effect she was trying to create.

Delphie painted the figures wearing different clothes to the ones in the photos. Her figure wore a dress that flowed beautifully in shades of pale yellow. She gave Wil a dark suit, white shirt and tie. The figures looked like them, while being part of the fantasy of the scene.

Every now and then she checked her phone for messages, having expected Gareth to contact her about her artwork for the show. Even just to acknowledge their meeting yesterday in Edinburgh. As the morning wore on and became lunchtime, she sighed. Some things really never changed. Gareth would be filled with enthusiasm for something, and then there would be silence from him.

But it was okay, she told herself. It left her free to work on the painting without interruption. And bolstered her resolve to push on with her own artwork.

Sienna refused to be persuaded that the original choreography was a winning routine, no matter how hard Wil tried. And he did try. Sienna and Steaphan had put a lot of effort into their routine, and Wil believed they could be successful. He couldn't say that as a couple they danced better than when he'd been partnered with Sienna. But they were an excellent pairing.

Miffed at Wil, Sienna left the dance studio under a cloud of disagreement. Steaphan paused to thank Wil for his efforts, and then hurried after her.

Wil let out the breath of frustration he'd been holding in. It was now late in the afternoon as the rehearsal had extended longer due to their bickering.

Securing the studio, Wil headed along to the grocery shop armed with his shopping list.

Carrying two full bags of groceries, including locally grown potatoes, carrots, turnip and other vegetables, raspberries, fresh cream for whipping and meringue cases, he loaded them into the back of his car and drove home to get showered and changed, and start preparing the dinner.

After showering, Wil put on a clean, light blue shirt, waistcoat and dark trousers. His hair was still damp and he swept it back from his clean–shaven face.

Hurrying downstairs, he checked that the already tidy house looked neat, and added plenty of logs to the fire. The house had central heating, but he liked the warmth of the real fire and the scent of the logs.

The hearty stew he'd made with lashings of gravy, onion and chunks of carrot, turnip and other vegetables, simmered on the stove. It wasn't as spicy as Kian's recipe. Just a tasty, homemade stew. Potatoes boiled in a second pot, ready for mashing.

While these cooked, he prepared the pudding. Whipping the cream into peaks, he spooned it on to two meringue cases and then added the fresh raspberries.

In reserve, if something went awry with his pudding plan, he'd bought a box of luxury chocolates that would suffice after they'd had their stew.

Hearing Delphie's car drive up, he checked the time. Perfect.

Feigning calm, he opened the front door to welcome her. 'Come in. Dinner's almost ready.'

Delphie wore a fashionable burgundy dress and heels, and hung her coat up in the hall, while Wil dashed through to the kitchen.

'Something smells delicious,' she said, following him through.

He stirred the stew and then drained the pot of potatoes.

'Can I help with anything?' she offered, noticing that he'd set the kitchen table with dinner plates, cutlery and napkins. He'd cut a plate of fresh bread. A vase of flowers plucked from his garden sat nearby. The effort he'd made warmed her heart.

'Could you make the tea while I mash the tatties,' he said.

Delphie started to pitch in, making the tea while Wil served up the stew and mash.

'Help yourself to salt and pepper, and add a knob of butter to your tatties if you want.'

Delphie added a dash of salt and black pepper. There was plenty of rich gravy with the stew. He'd chosen well.

'Tuck in,' he encouraged her.

She'd deliberately eaten a light lunch so she'd have an appetite for dinner.

'This is delicious, Wil. Is there anything you're not skilled at?' Her comment was jovial, but there was something that sprang to Wil's mind.

He wasn't great at expressing his feelings for her. But maybe tonight was a chance for him to try.

CHAPTER THIRTEEN

'I've always loved dancing,' Wil began as they enjoyed their dinner. 'When I was a wee boy, I loved going to the theatre to see dance shows more than films at the cinema. I remember the first time I saw a traditional ballet in one of the theatres in Edinburgh, and being in awe of the performers, and the ability to tell a story using only music and dance.'

Delphie nodded, listening to Wil while he continued.

'I attended dance classes when I was young, learning everything from ballet to ballroom,' he added. 'Then as I grew up and it was clear that I would make dancing my career, I always wanted to create my own show. Combining ballet with ballroom.'

Delphie blinked. 'A new show with ballet and ballroom dancing in it?'

'Yes. For years I toyed with various styles from traditional to modern stage elements,' Wil explained. 'I wrote down ideas, but that's all they remained while I forged on with my career. I was fortunate to take part in shows and contests all over the country and abroad. It gave me a wide perspective of what audiences liked.'

'And the music?'

'Ah, yes, that was always a key element,' Wil admitted. 'But a few years ago I met a composer, not much older than me, backstage after a performance. He asked me to keep him in mind if I ever wanted new music, classical in style. I kept in touch with him, and he's composed some wonderful pieces that I'm considering using for the show.'

'Was that the piano music I heard in the studio?'

'Yes, I've only ever told a few people about my dream to create a new show. It never seemed feasible until I came here. Having my own studio, making my own schedule, and meeting you.'

Delphie frowned. 'Meeting me?'

Wil reached over and lifted up his large notepad where he'd collected his ideas. He opened it at pages of sketches he'd made. 'These are some of my ideas for choreography. They look like chicken scratchings.'

Delphie laughed, but was interested to see his ideas. 'What's the theme of your show?'

'Again, that's something I've changed over the years. But since I bought your painting, The Sweetest Waltz, and met you, I've started to picture a theme of music, dance and romance.'

She looked through his notepad at the rough sketches.

Wil sighed heavily. 'I can't draw well enough to put together the visuals for each act in the show. The storyboard, the characters, as well as the dances have to be drawn by a capable artist, especially one with a background in dancing.'

Delphie's eyes widened as she gazed across at Wil. 'You want me to do the artwork?'

'I do. That's why I didn't tell you about it sooner. I wanted to make sure that I could do this before inviting you to join me in creating the show.'

Delphie felt her breath taken away by his offer.

'This isn't like Gareth's deal, even though I think the artwork you've done for him is excellent,' said Wil. 'This is a lot more. I need an artist with your talent to be part of the process. The composer has the music, and he aims to write other songs once the show's theme and story arc is finalised. I'll handle the choreography. I'd like you to draw the scenes for the show. To sketch the structure. Create a storyboard.'

The enormity of Wil's offer swept over her.

'You don't have to decide right now,' he assured her. 'There are other notebooks in the living room I'll let you have a browse through after dinner.'

Delphie heard what Wil was saying, but her mind whirled with the opportunity of a lifetime being offered to her. To be part of creating a new show. To work with Wil. To have her art at the core of it.

'I hope you'll help me rehearse the dance routines,' Wil added, piling on other aspects she'd love to do.

She felt as if her life shifted into the right groove for the first time in a long while. 'Yes,' she murmured.

Wil was so busy talking about his ideas, hoping to persuade her, that her acceptance didn't register with him.

'I'll let you hear the music that's been recorded after dinner too,' he said.

By now, they'd finished eating their main course. Wil stood up, lifted their plates over to the sink, and then served up the fruit and cream meringues.

'Yes,' Delphie repeated, gazing across at Wil.

He paused. 'You'll do it?'

'I will,' she confirmed.

A smile lit up his face. She smiled back at him.

Planning to discuss the details after dinner, they ate the meringues, both of them sensing that they were about to embark on something spectacular.

The time was right for Wil to make the ideas in his notebook real.

'We'll have to organise the party night at the barn,' he said, letting her know he hadn't forgotten it.

'And rehearse our waltz for the closing dance,' she said.

'We can do that.'

Yes, they could, she thought, confident that together they could do quite a few things.

She spooned up a mouthful of raspberries and cream.

Wil ate his too, eager to then go through to the living room to discuss their plans in front of the fire.

After they'd finished dinner, he grabbed his notebook and led her through to the living room.

'Can I sketch in your notepad?' said Delphie, flicking to blank pages near the back of it.

'Yes.' He was eager to see what she was going to draw.

Delphie dug into her bag and brought out a mechanical pencil that she used for her artwork and began to draw outlines for a storyboard. Across the top of the page she wrote bold lettering with the words *music*, *dance* and *romance*.

Wil went over and turned the composer's music on. 'This is a dramatic piano concerto. I thought it would be an ideal introduction to the show's opening scene. Obviously, I don't have the storyline yet.'

Delphie paused from sketching, relaxed back and listened to the beautiful music. 'Do you have any ideas for the storyline?'

Wil hesitated before explaining. 'Every time I look at The Sweetest Waltz painting hanging in my studio, I think about it being based on the old photograph of your grandparents. I'd love the storyline to be a romance from the past, with vintage costumes, and a happy ever after. The show would have to end on a happy note.'

Delphie pictured the figures in the painting. 'The lead couple could dance a romantic waltz on stage.'

'I can choreograph that, with help from you,' he said.

'Are we really going to try and make this work?'

'Yes, but you'll have to forgo a bit of your own plan.'

Delphie frowned. 'What do you mean?'

'That multitasker element will come in handy to get this show off the ground.'

'I never imagined I'd be any other type, so I think I can handle all the things we need to organise the show. Beginning with ideas for the scenery, the set designs, costumes, the whole atmosphere.'

'Don't forget the poster.'

'How could I have forgotten that,' she joked.

They sat together in front of the fire and started to make headway with the plan.

'I'm not suggesting we follow your grandparents' story exactly,' said Wil. 'Just the core elements, the sense of their first meeting, the challenges, the happy ever after. With their lifetime now mapped out, resulting in them having been together all these years, with dance at the heart of it.'

Delphie agreed, but her mind was already thinking of ideas that would create a fantasy of romance and dance. She explained this to Wil after asking him to replay the concerto.

'Listening to the power of this music, I'm picturing a dramatic opening scene,' said Delphie, letting her artistic imagination sketch what she had in mind for Wil to see.

He leaned close and watched as her sketches brought the atmosphere of the music to life, depicting the solitary figure of a young woman, a fantasy ballerina, descending down on to the stage amid an autumn scene.

'That would be a wonderful opening for Act One. I've always loved autumn settings. There's something magical about the scene amid the trees,' he said.

Delphie sketched the next little picture. 'She dances a solo number, to convey her feelings of isolation, on her own without any love in her life.' Delphie smiled wryly at Wil. 'You'll be able to portray this perfectly with your choreography.'

Wil grinned, liking that she was teasing him, challenging him.

The music reached a peak. 'This would be the perfect point to introduce the male lead dancer,' she said. 'The man destined to become the love of her life.'

Wil watched her draw a man, appearing from the side of the stage, admiring the ballerina from afar.

'And this would be their first meeting,' said Delphie. 'The night he falls in love with her.'

Wil's enthusiasm notched up. 'This would be a great start to the show in the first act.'

Delphie skipped to another blank page in the notebook and wrote *Act Two* at the top. 'We'll map out a rough arc and then gradually fill in the details.'

'It'll take time to create the whole storyline,' he acknowledged. 'I suppose you'll be back in Edinburgh by then. But with your quick trip there to meet Gareth, it wouldn't be too hard for us to continue working on this.'

'If anything, the lunch meeting showed me that it's more the thought that the city is so far away, when really it's not.' She almost added that she hadn't entirely decided whether she'd stay longer in the town or live in the farmhouse when her grandparents came home.

Wil nodded hopefully as she continued to draw.

'Act Two is where they start to fall deeply in love, but things happen to keep them apart,' said Delphie. She wrote the word *conflict* to fill in the blanks where there was no storyline.

'We'll add plenty of conflict to convey the drama,' said Wil, sounding as if he couldn't wait to get started.

Turning to another blank page, Delphie wrote *Act Three* across the notepad. 'I used to love reading stage plays, so I'm familiar with the structure. This would be our basic plan. Then we'd add as many *scenes* as we want into each act. The third act would culminate in the conflicts being resolved and the happy ever after ending.'

Wil liked Delphie's plan. 'You've made a complicated pipedream seem feasible.'

'Your choreography is the main key. And the music.'

'But your artwork has just brought the ideas to life.'

'All our strengths combined could make this work,' she said.

Another song started playing. A slow, romantic melody.

'This composition is one of my favourites,' said Wil. 'Perfect for a romantic waltz.'

'At the end of the show.'

'The couple could dance off into the sunshine, a happy future assured,' he added.

'Or dance under a starry sky,' Delphie suggested. 'I've painted the couple dancing under the stars in front of the farmhouse.'

Wil perked up. 'Is it finished?'

'Not yet, but I took you up on your idea. I'm painting it in acrylics on canvas.'

'I'd love to see it.'

'Pop round to the barn any time.'

'Would tomorrow night suit?' he suggested.

'It would.'

'We could rehearse the closing waltz for the party night.'

'That would be sensible. The time is whizzing in. I haven't even moved my art studio into the farmhouse.'

'I'll help you do that tomorrow evening,' he offered.

'In exchange for dinner,' she insisted.

'It's a date.' This time he didn't correct himself.

Delphie smiled warmly, and then started to sketch more ideas on the notepad.

Wil went over to a drawer and brought out a new pad. 'At the rate you're drawing, you'll need a blank one.'

Delphie accepted it. 'Right, what other ideas have you jotted down?' She searched through the pages of his rough plans.

Wil began to explain his scribbled notes, hoping they made sense. There were key words. A reminder that he wanted to include a full waltz with several couples dancing on stage. Elements of fantasy mixed in with true romance. He heard himself try to rationalise the jumble of jottings.

They made total sense to Delphie.

Once again, she'd exceeded his expectations by a country mile.

'More tea?' Wil offered as the evening wore on.

'Yes, please,' she chirped, sounding as if she wasn't the least bit tired. It was more like she was fired up with enthusiasm, sketching the storyboard and chatting to Wil about the new show.

While listening to Wil rattling the cups in the kitchen, creating a feeling of homeliness, she worked on their plan. It looked like a series of boxed images, the lines neat, drawn by hand. Each piece played out the story, scene by scene, with sketches to indicate a dance sequence, written notes, or left blank where the missing parts of the show's jigsaw would be slotted in later.

The process reminded her so much of her graphic design work when she'd been tasked to prepare a visual presentation of a client's marketing plan. So much of it was second nature to her. Again, her past came to the fore when she needed it for future projects. Though she never imagined she'd be designing the storyboard for Wil's dancing dream.

Her own dream of dancing on stage had led her to read stage plays. To study the structure. She'd wanted to learn how characters were developed throughout the performance. How scenery and settings were described. The side notes were a wealth of fascinating information, and she'd gleaned an insight into the structure of the acts and scenes. She'd picked them up in bookshops, and her grandmother had a collection on a shelf in the farmhouse kitchen, alongside recipe, sewing, quilting and knitting books. And there was a folder where her grandmother had kept the original copies of the scripts from stage shows she'd performed in. All of these had scribbled notes in the margins. They provided an amazing slice of the past, now relevant in the present. Delphie planned to check them when she went back to the farmhouse, but for now, she was relying on what she'd already learned.

While the kettle boiled, Wil set up a tea tray, balancing the box of luxury chocolates he'd bought on the side of it. He didn't think he needed to sweeten Delphie up. She was the sweetest natured person he'd ever met, determined too. The perfect blend. Nice, but nobody's fool. Except when it came to Gareth. Pushing this thought aside, he made the tea and carried the tray through to the living room.

'Luxury chocolates?' Delphie exclaimed. 'Hmmm, you're really pulling out all the stops this evening.'

'They were sitting on the kitchen's reserve bench in case my meringues went awry.'

Delphie giggled. 'It would be a shame to let these truffles go to waste.'

'There's no chance of that this evening,' he said, opening the box and giving her first dibs of the dark chocolate truffles.

CHAPTER FOURTEEN

It was another night when Delphie felt reluctant to leave the cosy fireside at Wil's house to head back to the farmhouse. But it was late, and they'd made huge progress with their plans for the new show.

Delphie closed the notebook and handed it to Wil. 'It's been an exciting evening, but it's getting late.'

'Thank you for helping with the artwork and the ideas for the show,' said Wil, walking her out to the hall and helping her on with her coat.

He opened the front door and they felt the cold air blow in.

'I'll see you tomorrow night,' she said.

'Yes, I'll come by when I've finished at the studio.'

Delphie nodded and hurried out to her car.

As before, he waved as she drove off, feeling less inclined to let her go each time.

Delphie glanced in the mirror, seeing Wil standing there lit up in the warm glow of the doorway. Her heart ached a little as she drove away.

Arriving at the farmhouse, she hurried inside and prepared herself for a restless night. She knew how her mind sparked with ideas when tasked with making plans, designs or artwork.

Grabbing a notebook of her own, she took it upstairs and sat it on the bedside table along with a pencil, quite prepared to have her slumber interspersed with jotting down ideas for the show's storyboard.

Before she'd even snuggled under the covers, she sat up in bed and made notes.

Wil sat by the heat of the fire's embers reading the notebook. The storyboard sketches brought the show to life, and he found himself thinking of choreography for some of the dances they'd talked about.

But it was getting late, and he'd yet another busy day at the studio, so he put the notebook aside, turned the lights off in the living room, and headed upstairs to bed.

Unlike Delphie, he slept right through to the morning.

Delphie worked on the starry sky painting in the barn during the day, finishing it, and then got ready for Wil arriving that evening.

The farmhouse kitchen felt cosy as she checked on the roast potatoes in the oven and served up two salmon pasties made with puff pastry, garden peas sprinkled with chives, and a spoonful of cranberry sauce.

Wil had sent a message from the dance studio that he was on his way and would be there in a few minutes.

Delphie made a pot of tea and set their cups up as Wil knocked on the door.

'Come on in,' she called to him.

Wil walked through to the kitchen and smiled when he saw her. 'Dinner looks tasty,' he said, seeing their plates on the table as he went over to the sink to wash his hands.

Delphie poured their tea. 'The roast potatoes should be ready soon.'

The oven pinged, and Wil pitched in, grabbed the oven gloves and lifted the tray of sizzling roast potatoes out and helped to serve them up. 'I love roasties,' he said.

Sitting down at the table, they chatted about the party night.

'Kian phoned today to tell me that all the tickets are sold,' said Delphie. 'He's arranged to come up to the barn to organise the drinks for the bar and a few other things.'

'I've brought a music playlist that I use for the studio. We should listen to that this evening and agree what songs we want to use.'

Delphie felt a rush of excitement charge through her. 'And we need to rehearse our waltz.' She'd worn a dress and heels for dancing.

'I'll help you move your artwork into the farmhouse after dinner, and clear the floor so we can dance.' He smiled at her. 'Thanks for making dinner. It's delicious.' He ate another roast potato and tucked into the pastry.

Delphie enjoyed her meal too, and liked the easy rhythm between them as they sat together in the kitchen chatting over dinner.

They'd agreed the previous night that Wil's plan to create his own show wouldn't be a secret now. So she'd told her grandparents earlier in the day.

'My grandparents are thrilled that The Sweetest Waltz painting was the spark that ignited the storyboard for the show. And that parts of their background will be incorporated into the dances.'

Wil smiled as he continued to eat his dinner, pleased that her grandparents were happy.

'My gran suggested that we could use some of her vintage dresses for the styling of the costumes.'

'That's a great idea.'

'I've had a browse through her wardrobes and added a couple of designs to the storyboard.'

Wil grinned.

'I know,' she said. 'But you encouraged me to multitask.'

Wil finished his dinner. 'I did, but let's double up on the tasks tonight. I'll start moving the artwork.'

'I'll clear the dishes and show you where I want my art studio set up.'

Agreeing to make short work of this, Delphie led Wil through to the room where she'd cleared a space for her easels and paints.

It didn't take Wil long to lift her artwork from the barn into the farmhouse. Delphie helped, organising her watercolour paints, oils and acrylics into the dresser and drawers her grandmother used for crafting.

He admired her starry sky painting that was now displayed on an easel. 'You've really captured the feeling of a night sky, and I recognise the farmhouse. The couple dancing are familiar too.' He grinned knowingly.

'The figures are from our quickstep video. But I added different clothes for artistic flair.'

'What are you going to do with it?' he said.

'I thought I'd keep it as a memento of my time here.'

Wil nodded, jarred once again by the time stamp of her leaving.

Heading back over to the barn, Wil checked the music system and added his playlist.

They spent the next few minutes agreeing on the songs to play at the start of the party night. Then Wil suggested a couple of songs for their ending waltz.

He played the first song and took Delphie in hold. 'This is a classic. I'm sure you know it.'

'I do know it. It's a lovely romantic song.'

Under the twinkle lights, they waltzed around, deciding if this song was better, or the second choice.

'The second song would suit a waltz with more flair,' said Delphie.

'It would, but there's nothing to beat a true classic, a traditional waltz danced well.' Wil gazed down at her, still keeping her close in hold. 'And the first song is so romantic.'

'We should use the first one,' Delphie agreed, hoping he didn't sense the effect his closeness had on her.

'I'll play it again from the beginning.' He hurried over and reset it, then came back and held her in a traditional hold.

And then they danced around the floor, matching each other's movements as if they'd rehearsed it several times.

'This waltz suits us,' Wil said as they circled the floor.

'It does,' she agreed. 'I was thinking I'd wear one of my grandmother's dresses to add to the performance.'

'Perfect. I'll wear a classic suit.'

They continued to practise their routines, and set things up in the barn ready for the party.

Wil climbed up a step ladder to adjust the spotlights over the dance floor, angling them as if he was setting up a stage performance.

Delphie looked up the old video of her grandparents dancing when they were young that she'd used for The Sweetest Waltz painting.

Wil heard the song lyrics and climbed down to watch the video. 'They dance so well together.'

'They do.' Delphie felt Wil's closeness and her heart reacted stronger than ever. But she kept her conversation light to disguise the depths of her feelings. 'My grandmother kept the dress. It's hanging in the wardrobe.'

'Are you going to wear it for our waltz?' he said hopefully.

Delphie glanced up at him. 'I thought I would. I've never worn it. I'd need to try it on. But the wardrobes are filled with other dresses.'

'I'd like to see them. As you said, they could be handy for designing the costumes for our show.'

Our show. The words resonated through her. But it was true. They were creating the show together.

Wil put the ladder away, satisfied that the spotlights were sorted.

Leaving the barn, they walked together towards the farmhouse. Wil suddenly paused and clasped her hand.

'Dance with me,' he said playfully, gazing up at the stars in the night sky shining above them.

Delphie smiled and began dancing with him.

'I want to feel what it would be like for the couple in the painting,' he said.

The low cut grass added a softness to their steps, but they danced smoothly as he held her close.

'Nature's dance floor feels great,' she said, letting Wil lead them around for a few moments before they went into the farmhouse.

'Would you like to see the vintage dresses?' Delphie offered.

'Lead the way.'

Upstairs, Delphie opened the wardrobes doors. 'My grandmother kept these beautiful dresses that she wore for dancing. Even the ones after she stopped dancing professionally.'

Wil looked impressed. 'It's an amazing collection.'

Delphie unhooked the beautiful pink dress and held it up in front of herself to show him.

Wil stepped forward and instinctively reached out to touch the fabric, feeling the gorgeous silk chiffon of the dress that was depicted in his painting. 'So, this is the dress from The Sweetest Waltz.'

'It is.' Delphie turned to look at her reflection in the mirror while holding up the dress. 'It would be lovely to wear it for our waltz at the party night.'

'Wear it,' he said. 'It's perfect.'

Delphie nodded, planning to try it on later, and then hung it back up in the wardrobe.

She showed him various dresses, each one a vintage classic design.

'These would add authenticity to our show if the costumes were based on them,' he said, and singled one out. 'This lilac dress looks like something out of a fairytale.'

Delphie lifted the wispy chiffon and silk creation from the wardrobe and let Wil have a closer look. 'My grandmother made these dresses,' she revealed.

Wil blinked. 'She stitched these herself?'

'Yes, she trained as a dressmaker in Paris and worked in French couture while she was a dancer.'

'I noticed the sewing machine in the kitchen.'

'Sewing is her hobby now, but...' Delphie tried to reach a box from the top shelf of one of the wardrobes.

Wil lifted it down for her and watched as she opened it to reveal tidily folded paper patterns that her grandmother had made to create the dresses.

'These are her patterns. She kept them all, and the dresses. There is so much more to the clothes than mementos of wearing them for dancing. She's a skilled dressmaker and even the sequins and beading are her handiwork.'

Wil looked thoughtful. 'Do you think your grandmother would be interested in helping us with the show's costume designs?'

Delphie's eyes lit up. 'Oh, I'm sure she'd love to do that.' She pictured her grandmother's excitement of coming home to help design the dresses.

'Thank you, Wil.'

'For what?' he said.

'Just for being you.'

He smiled warmly, and they continued to sift through the dresses and the patterns, and talked more about the storyline for the show.

'Romance is at the heart of it,' he insisted. 'Despite the conflict, true romance needs to be the thread running through it.'

'I should write some of these ideas down on the storyboard,' said Delphie.

Tidying up the wardrobes, they went downstairs and while Delphie made the tea, Wil popped out to his car and came back in with the notebook plans.

'I brought this with me, just in case we needed it,' he said, putting it down on the kitchen table.

Delphie grabbed a pencil and jotted down the things they'd just discussed.

Wil made the tea while she did this.

Sitting down at the kitchen table, they talked about the plans for the show.

Delphie stopped suddenly and put her pencil down. 'Our focus should be on the party night,' she reminded them firmly.

'We've got everything ready for the party that we need at the moment,' he said calmly.

'You're right.' Delphie picked up her pencil and continued to add to the storyboard.

Finally calling it a night, Delphie walked Wil out.

'I'll pop into the bakery shop in the morning,' he said. 'I'll talk to Kian and Catriona, and see if there's anything else we need to get ready.'

Waving to each other, Wil drove off home and Delphie went inside the farmhouse and got ready for bed.

Switching off the lights downstairs, she noticed the starry sky painting sitting on the easel in her relocated art studio.

Equipped with a hammer and nails, she put it up on the wall in her bedroom beside the original painting of her grandparents outside the farmhouse. Side by side, they showed her progression from a budding artist to an accomplished one.

Lying in bed, moonlight streamed through the window, shining a beam across the two paintings. Thinking about her art, her evening with Wil, waltzing with him in the barn, and giving him a peek at the dresses, she drifted off to sleep.

Wil sat at a window table with Kian in the bakery shop, deep in conversation, as Catriona served up two teas and a roll filled with scrambled eggs and grilled tomatoes for Wil.

Kian had his notes and tick boxed down the to–do list. 'That's most things done, except the actual setting up of the bar and buffet on the night. But Catriona and I have part–time staff and other folk eager to muck in. So all is fine.'

Wil saw his own face frowning, reflected in the window, in stark contrast to Kian's cheery demeanour.

'Relax, Wil,' Kian told him. 'We've got your back. The town has your back. Everyone's happy that the party night is on this year. We're up to our eyeballs in folk popping in saying they'd like to help.'

'It's a great community.'

'Now get your breakfast down you,' Kian insisted.

Wil lifted up his roll and took a bite, feeling his appetite instantly remedied by the delicious filling.

Catriona hurried over. 'I've just had the lads from the local band on the phone. They're offering to play during the party night.'

It transpired that they were the three men, two fiddlers and an accordionist from the ceilidh night at the hotel.

'They usually play at the barn parties. I told them you've organised a playlist of dance music, but they'll play two or three numbers halfway through the evening,' Catriona explained to Wil. 'I said yes. I hope that's okay.'

'Yes, that's more than okay,' Wil agreed. 'They were a lively band and seemed popular.'

'They are,' Kian added. 'We'll pay them a wee bit out of the ticket sales.'

With a live band now part of the party, and with the town eager to participate, Wil saw his frown fade in the reflection, and tucked into his breakfast.

In the afternoon, Delphie watched the barn being transformed at speed. Barrels of beer were connected up ready for pouring and bottles of everything from whisky to wine were stocked on the shelves behind the bar. Kian and his helpers prepared the bar and buffet area, insisting she stand aside so they could make short work of it. Delphie kept out of their way so as not to be a hindrance.

Watching the barn buzzing with activity, Delphie's excitement soared, and made her want to be part of this town's close–knit community more than ever. The smiling faces, the laughter as they worked together to set up something that everyone would enjoy, warmed her heart.

She kept in touch with Wil, whizzing messages back and forth, as he was working on helping dancers online with their choreography.

And Delphie had received a message from Gareth that everything was going smoothly with her artwork for his project in Edinburgh. He'd added that Sienna and Steaphan were competing in the contest later in the city.

Do you think Sienna and Steaphan will win? Delphie wondered what Gareth thought of their chances.

I think so. Sienna is confident in their choreography. Wil did a great job, but she's added her own special flair.

As the afternoon wore on, and the buzzing calmed to a gentle murmur of activity, Kian and the others finally headed away. Delphie thanked them profusely, and it seemed that people were looking forward to seeing her dancing with Wil, and having a fun night.

Her grandmother called to say that she was having a romantic dinner in Paris, and Delphie took the opportunity to tell her about the costume designing.

'Oh, yes! Tell Wil I'd be happy to help you with the designs,' said her grandmother. 'And your grandfather and I are so excited that you're planning a new show with Wil.'

'We expect front row seats to the opening night performance,' her grandfather chimed–in cheerily.

'I promise you'll have them,' said Delphie.

After the call, Delphie headed over to the farmhouse and went upstairs to try the pink dress on.

It fitted as if it was made for her, and she tried on her dance shoes with it. Looking in the mirror, she saw a variation of her grandmother from yesteryear. Taking it off and hanging it up ready for the party night, she then put on the lilac dress that Wil had so admired. It fitted well too, and it did look like something from a fairytale. Deciding she'd wear it for their opening dance, the quickstep, she hung it up, closed the wardrobe doors and went downstairs to make dinner.

CHAPTER FIFTEEN

While dinner cooked, Delphie wandered through to where her artwork was set up in the farmhouse, picked out a blank canvas and sat it on one of the easels. Taking a pencil suitable for drawing on the primed surface of the stretched canvas, she drew a dancing couple.

Callum had contacted her, wanting more dance theme paintings for his art shop. She'd promised him she'd work on them.

The lilac dress had given her ideas for her paintings, and this one featured the fairytale dress being worn as the couple danced together in the scene. The lilac tones of the dress would merge with midnight violets and lavender hues in the background, and she pictured adding starlight to create a fantasy feel.

With the sketch drawn on the canvas, Delphie selected the colours of acrylics she'd use for her palette, planning to make a start on the painting after dinner.

Wil listened to the composer's music as he danced around the studio. Wil had spoken to him earlier on a video call, and heard the latest piece of music being played on a baby grand piano. He'd sent Wil a copy, and they'd discussed its inclusion in the new show.

The romantic rhapsody resonated in the studio, igniting ideas for the choreography. The storyboard that Delphie had drawn helped him visualise a dramatic scene where the two lead characters were dancing. Maybe later, he'd drop by the farmhouse and ask Delphie to dance it with him.

Although he knew it would take a while to put a show like this together, each dance he choreographed pushed it closer to completion. He was determined to keep making progress with it, especially as Delphie worked so fast. Between the two of them, and the composer's enthusiasm, he believed they could do this.

During a break in the afternoon, he'd ventured down the shore to get some fresh sea air and take time to clear his thoughts.

No swimming today, but he enjoyed the walk along the quiet stretch of sand. The sea sparkled like liquid silver in the afternoon light. Way off in the distance, boats sailed along the silvery horizon.

The air bore a hint of autumn, but this didn't deter Wil from planning to go swimming there on other days and inviting Delphie to join him.

Heading back to the studio he felt refreshed, and was delighted when a friend of his phoned to ask if Wil would help him with the dance choreography for a theatre show in Edinburgh. Wil scheduled for them to come down to the studio later in the month to rehearse. His friend ran the theatre and Wil had performed there a few times. Set in Edinburgh, Wil loved that it was tucked into a niche that looked like it belonged to the past. A hidden gem.

After dinner, Delphie worked on the painting. Adding more crimson and cobalt blue to her palette, she painted the background, sweeping a larger brush across the skyline to cover the canvas, while outlining the figures.

Wil had sent a message asking if he could drop by when he finished up at the studio. So after completing the first layer of the background, she left it to dry and got ready for him arriving.

He wanted to try out some new choreography, so she'd changed into a dress and put her dancing shoes on.

She'd just put the kettle on for tea when she saw Wil's car headlights illuminating the garden.

He arrived, bringing a copy of the rhapsody on his phone and ideas for the choreography.

Delphie made the tea while he told her about the new piece of music.

Pouring two cups of tea, she invited him to play the rhapsody. They sat sipping their tea and listening to the song's romantic melody fill the kitchen.

'That's so beautiful. It has to be a lead piece for the show.'

'Or part of the romantic finale,' Wil suggested.

'Yes,' said Delphie, picturing a fairytale waltz amid a wonderful setting. She sighed. 'I wish I could watch it right now. It's been a hectic but productive day.'

Wil told her he'd meandered down the shore.

'Did you go in for a swim?'

'No, I just wanted a walk in the fresh air. But I hope you'll join me for a dip in the sea another day while there's still some heat in the sunshine.'

Delphie nodded.

Wil then told her about his friend wanting him to help with the dance choreography for the theatre in Edinburgh. 'Do you know the theatre? It's tucked into a niche.'

'That's the wee theatre hidden in the heart of the city,' she said. 'I've never been to any shows there, but I've walked past it, barely knowing it was there.'

'It has a fair capacity due to the depth of the structure. The stage and the interior reminds me of stepping into a storybook from the past. They've kept the original structure and updated the decor with vintage styling. I love the atmosphere of it,' he said. 'I told him about our new dance show, and he says we're welcome to rehearse on the stage when we're ready.'

'That would be handy. The dance studio is great, but an actual theatre would be ideal for rehearsing the show.'

'We could hold our opening night there. The seating capacity is a lot more than the impression the small theatre gives at first glance.'

While they were chatting, a message came through for Delphie from Gareth. It was short and bittersweet.

Sienna and Steaphan didn't win the contest.

Delphie replied. *Thanks for letting me know, Gareth.*

She told Wil the news.

Wil already knew. 'Steaphan called me. They didn't even place in the top three. They were fourth.'

Delphie winced. 'Sienna won't be happy.'

'Nooo,' said Wil. 'Steaphan told me they got into a fankle with a couple of the new moves Sienna added to the routine.'

Moving on from the news, they finished their tea, and Delphie showed Wil the painting she was working on.

'I've only painted part of the background,' she explained. 'I'm planning to include the lilac dress and create a fairytale atmosphere.'

Wil admired her work.

'Callum wants more dance theme artwork, acrylics and watercolours,' she said. 'This canvas will be a limited edition print sold from the art shop website.'

'From what I can see of the colours so far, this painting will look wonderful as a print.'

Then they headed over to the barn to listen to the rhapsody and practise the choreography he'd been working on.

The barn looked like a venue for a night of entertainment, with the spotlights and twinkle lights illuminating the dance floor and bar area. Seeing it like this brought back a flood of memories to Delphie and she was looking forward to being part of the fun.

Wil tapped the dance floor and glanced around him. 'There's an energy about the barn, even when we're the only couple here.'

Referring to them as a couple resonated through her. As the opening notes of the rhapsody filtered out from his phone, it felt like they were embarking on being a real couple, not just dancing acquaintances, or teaming up to create a show. More than that. Much more. The feelings she had for Wil were deepening every time she danced with him, and as he gently pulled her into his arms when the romantic melody began, she knew how easy it would be to fall in love with him.

Secretly mirroring her feelings as they danced, he shook away the temptation to overstep the line between friendship and intimacy. This wasn't the time or the place to declare his growing affection for her.

Following his lead, she matched his steps, flowing into the choreography as if they'd already danced it together.

'You're more in tune with me than anyone I've ever danced with,' he said, and then spun her around the floor, taking her breath away with his strength, poise and aptitude for dancing a classic waltz.

He stopped and rewound the song. 'I'd like to try a variation on a few of the sequences.' He showed her what he had in mind. She picked up on these, and they danced again, this time adding more flair to the routine.

'I like this routine,' she told him when they paused.

'You dance so well,' he said, gazing down at her. 'There's a balletic quality to some of your moves that suits my style of dancing.'

The way he looked at her set her senses alight.

Blinking out of the temptation to kiss her, he continued to choreograph the dance.

He took her by surprise with a finishing move that swept her off her feet as he wrapped his arm around her waist and lifted her off the floor as he continued to spin.

Delphie giggled breathlessly as he put her down.

He smiled at her reaction. 'Sorry, I should've told you about that finishing move.'

She smiled. 'Well, I think you should include it.'

Playfully, he reached out to her. 'What if I were to lift you even higher.'

Delphie darted away, laughing. 'No, Wil, no!'

Chasing after her, he caught her before she made a bolt for the door, and lifted her up with ease, strong but gentle, before setting her down again.

She swiped at him jokingly. 'I don't believe that was part of the choreography.'

Wil shrugged. 'Sometimes, you bring out the rascal in me.'

Delphie gasped. 'Only sometimes?'

And then the chase was on again.

The two of them finally called it a draw, both breathless from laughing.

'Is this how you usually teach people your choreography?' she said lightly.

'No, this is only when I'm with you.' His voice dipped and took on a deeper tone. 'Only with you.'

She felt the romantic tension between them, but there were so many things still unsettled in her life, and falling for Wil would change everything even more. The timing wasn't right, especially as the party was only two nights away.

Wil sensed her hesitancy, and reigned in his own longing. But he knew there would come a time soon when he'd tell her how he felt.

A message on Wil's phone jarred them. Then another message.

Delphie stepped back as he checked them.

'Word is getting around about Sienna and Steaphan's performance at the contest,' he told her.

His phone started to light up with messages.

'I'll let you deal with this,' said Delphie, prepared to end their evening there.

Wil frowned as he read them. 'A few of the dancers I've been working with are keen to hear my thoughts.'

'They're not blaming you, are they?'

'No, quite the opposite. They think Sienna was foolish to change the choreography.'

'We've surely rehearsed enough for this evening.' Delphie started to turn the lights off in the barn.

Wil was torn, but he could see that Delphie seemed fine with this, so he made his way out of the barn.

As he walked to his car, he paused and glanced back. 'Would you like to go swimming with me in the morning?'

'Okay. What time?'

'Crack of dawn. We'll have the shore all to ourselves.'

Delphie feigned disappointment. 'But then no one will see me beating you in a race along the shore.'

'Are you talking about swimming or sprinting?'

'Take your pick,' she joked in a challenging tone.

'I choose both,' he said, smiling defiantly.

'Beaten twice in the one day. Are you up for that?'

Wil burst out laughing. 'I trust you're winding me up.'

Delphie smiled sweetly, giving him no such assurance. Though she doubted she could beat Wil at all. But the gauntlet had been thrown down.

Wil nodded his acceptance. 'Swimwear and sandshoes at dawn.'

Wil picked Delphie up in the morning as the sky above the farmhouse had barely cracked a ray of dawn. But she'd slept well and was up for the trip down the shore. She wore black dance leggings and a long sleeve top over her pink swimsuit, training shoes, and had pinned her hair up in a top knot.

She threw the bag she'd packed with her towel in the back seat of his car, and jumped in the front as Wil drove off. He looked like he was ready for action, wearing a tight–fitting black top and black joggers.

'Sleep well?' he said. 'Or were you up all night planning how to thwart me?'

'I slept sound. And I have a plan. Run like blazes and swim like a shark.'

'No wonder I couldn't sleep,' he joked.

Teasing each other, they soon arrived down the shore. No one else was there. Not even a distant ship on the flat calm horizon.

They got out of the car and Delphie limbered up, squinting against the sunlight that was now shining through the cloudy dawn and reflecting off the silvery sea.

'Do you want to run or swim first?' he said, looking like he could take on all challengers with his tall, fit build.

'Run. Then you can ease off your tired muscles in the salt water.'

'Oh, you're in big trouble young lady,' Wil said, finding her chirpy confidence warm his heart. Unlike the cold sea was due to do. But he pushed this thought aside and got ready to run.

Delphie picked up a piece of driftwood and drew a line in the clean sand.

The tide was far out, leaving the light sand smooth and compact, and quite good for running on. This area of the shore wasn't rocky or scattered with pebbles, seashells or sea glass, just a vast expanse of sand.

'We'll make that the finishing line,' she said, beginning to walk away to where they'd start sprinting. 'Roughly a one hundred metre dash.'

'Going for speed, huh?'

'I can extend it if you want, give you a chance to catch up.'

He laughed, hearing his voice filter into the fresh sea air.

'No, a hundred metres suits me. I'm usually quick off the mark.'

He'd barely uttered these words when Delphie dashed off, leaving Wil gasping at her opportunistic tactics. 'That's cheating!'

Her giggling trailed behind her, along with Wil, unable to catch up, mainly from her unexpected fast start and laughing.

Delphie raced across the finishing line and lifted her arms up in triumph.

Wil hadn't even had a chance to take his phone from his trouser pocket before the race, but he used it to take a snap of her triumph. Everything about the photo showed Delphie filled with energy, smiling with joy, and it would surely be one of his favourite pictures of her.

Letting out a huge sigh of relief and breathlessness, she smiled at him. 'Even if you win at the swimming, the most you can achieve is a draw with me.'

'Fair enough,' he conceded, stripping off his outer clothing to reveal his swimming trunks and a body that was a total distraction.

Delphie tried not to look like she was admiring him, but Wil was fit. She knew this from the last time, but seeing him standing there, lean muscles ready to challenge her, set her heartbeat haywire.

She took her things off and walked down towards the sea in her swimsuit.

They agreed where they'd swim to, turn and head back.

The sea looked cold, but Delphie told herself not to think about it and just get in there and start swimming.

Wading in, she gasped. 'It seems colder than I remember.'

'Running like blazes has probably warmed you up, so it seems colder by comparison.'

Delphie gave him a doubtful side–eye.

'Okay, maybe it's a bit brisker than before,' he said.

Diving under the surface in tandem, they set off with Wil taking the lead, though Delphie's technique of going all out from the start placed her in a close enough second.

Wil reached the turning marker ahead of her, but Delphie was enjoying the race, and that's what mattered most to him. The fun they had together.

With Wil winning with more ease than Delphie's all–out effort, he lifted her up in triumph.

'Don't drop me in the water,' she squealed at him from his shoulder height.

Pretending he was going to do just that, he then caught her in his strong arms and placed her down gently.

She splashed him and scolded him, resulting in Wil running out of the sea and being chased by a giggling Delphie.

Retrieving her towel from her bag, she wrapped it around her, shivering slightly, but feeling invigorated.

Wil shook the droplets of water from his hair, swept it back from his face and smiled at her. 'A draw?'

Delphie extended her hand and they shook on it.

His fingers wrapped around her hand and he then clasped her close to him and began a makeshift waltz.

The wet muscles of his physique pressed against the fabric of her swimsuit, and she could feel every bit of his strength to her core.

Delphie glanced around to see that they still had the shore all to themselves. No one else was there to see two fools dancing on the shore as the dawn sunlight shone through the morning sky.

Leaving her for a moment, he hurried over to his car and came back with a rucksack and two blankets. He wrapped one blanket around Delphie to shield her from the cold and put the other one down on the sand.

Patting himself dry with a towel, he shrugged his top on and sat down beside her. Pouring two hot cups of tea from a flask, he handed one to her.

She cupped it gladly, and they sat together gazing out at the glistening sea.

They sat there chatting happily about their dancing, their plans for the party and the show, finishing off two cups each. And then Wil drove them home.

It was still early morning by the time Delphie got out of the car outside the farmhouse.

'That was fun,' she said.

'It was,' he agreed. 'I'll see you later, and let me know if you need my help with anything today for the barn.'

Nodding, she waved him off and then went in to shower and get dressed.

Delphie spent the day getting on with her artwork, making progress with the acrylic painting and watercolours.

She sat outside in the garden to have a cup of tea and a piece of shortbread in the afternoon. Sunlight deceivingly gave the impression that it was the height of summer, but some of the leaves on the trees had a tint of autumn gold and bronze, giving a more accurate assessment of the season.

The party night celebration seemed appropriate now that the summer blooms were giving way to the autumn florals.

With most of the party preparations well in hand for the following evening, the day felt like the calm before the storm of organising the catering and getting ready for the dancing.

But it gave her time to think even more about living in the town and not going back to Edinburgh, except for short trips. She'd tentatively dropped a couple of heavy hints during a recent chat to her grandparents that she was thinking of extending her stay at the farmhouse. They'd been delighted. Now that she was working on the new show with Wil and involving her grandmother in the costume designs, it was surely more convenient to live in the town.

That prospect led to thoughts of Wil. It was clear that they were becoming closer.

And the demand for her art was greater than it had been when she worked in the city.

Finishing her tea, she went inside to continue working on her paintings.

Wil had succumbed to lunch at the bakery shop, and chatted to Kian and Catriona about any last minute plans for the party. They had the catering organised, and Kian planned to drive up to the barn the following day in his van loaded with enough food to fill the buffet.

Wil noticed a buzz in the town as people were looking forward to the event. And it felt like he'd become part of the community.

In the afternoon he had video calls from dancers learning choreography, and his plan to instruct them from the studio was working well.

But thoughts of Delphie kept filtering through his mind, knowing he was falling in love with her.

Locking up the studio to head home for dinner, Wil noticed Kian waving frantically to him from the bakery shop window. Wil hurried over to see what was wrong.

Kian handed him a white cardboard box as Wil walked in.

'I was cooking up new recipes for the buffet,' said Kian. 'Here's samples to take away with you. There are mini quiche, two slices of a cheese and vegetable bake, wee sausage rolls, and a couple of wedges of apple and bramble pie. I thought you'd like to try them. There's no chance you'll get a nibble tomorrow night at the party. These will go like hotcakes, and you and Delphie will be so busy dancing and tending to your guests, you'll be lucky to get a sniff of a biscuit.'

Kian was joking, but Wil was glad to take the samples. 'This will save me cooking dinner.'

'Enjoy,' said Kian, waving him off.

Getting into his car, Wil sent a message to Delphie.
Have you had dinner?
No, I'm thinking about raiding the freezer.
Don't. Kian has plied me with samples from the buffet. There's more than enough for two.
I'll put the kettle on.

Wil arrived at the farmhouse armed with the box of buffet delights. He put it down on the kitchen table.

Delphie opened it and peered in. 'Oh, this looks tempting.'

Helping Delphie set up the plates and cutlery, they chatted about their day.

'I had a bowl of soup for lunch and a piece of shortbread for afternoon tea,' said Delphie. 'Somehow, I skipped breakfast, but I do remember swimming in the sea.'

'I had lunch at the bakery shop, but I've certainly got an appetite. I've danced my socks off all day.'

Sitting down to the makeshift buffet, they shared the tasty treats.

Finishing up, Wil wondered if Delphie would like to rehearse their dances for the party. 'It'll be the last chance we get to practise the quickstep and our waltz.'

'Okay, I'll change my shoes,' she said.

Walking over to the barn she breathed in deeply. 'There's a scent of autumn in the air.'

'I love the autumn. I hear the town looks great at this time of year.'

'Yes, the farmhouse blends in with the burnished colours of the trees, flowers and scenery.'

Inside the barn, Wil set up their quickstep music.

Beginning in promenade hold, they stepped with flair into the opening beat, dancing across the diagonal, and then covering the dance floor with fast flicks and spins.

Finishing in time to the music, they agreed they'd nailed the choreography.

'For a fast dance, it feels intuitive dancing with you,' said Delphie.

'We dance well together,' he agreed, walking over to change the music for their waltz.

The romance of the song resonated around them as they began to dance.

Delphie knew the atmosphere would feel less intimate when they had an audience. But tonight, it was just the two of them, and she loved the feeling of being in Wil's capable arms as they waltzed.

As the music ended, and the final notes drifted out of the barn into the night air, she wanted to remember these moments with Wil.

Deciding it made more sense to end the night there, Delphie walked back to the farmhouse, waving as Wil drove home.

Although tempted to paint or sketch into the late night, Delphie did the sensible thing and got ready for bed so she was well rested for the busy day ahead.

Wil decided to do the same, but before getting into bed, he checked his wardrobe to make sure the classic suit that he planned to wear for the party was hanging up ready. It was, along with his white ballroom stretch shirts and ties.

He turned off the bedside lamp and lay there gazing out the window at the night sky and fell asleep rewinding the dances with Delphie.

The following day flew by in a flurry of activity, especially the late afternoon as Kian, Catriona and their assistants set up the buffet in the barn.

Wil had made himself available during the day to help with anything that was needed, but now as the twilight's glow stretched across the sky, he'd gone home to get changed into his suit.

Delphie put on the lilac dress and checked her hair and makeup in the mirror. Butterflies of excitement fluttered through her as she hurried downstairs to head over to the barn.

The solar lights in the farmhouse driveway flickered into life in time for the stream of car headlights approaching in the distance.

Here they come, Delphie thought, watching their arrival in the golden hour glow.

It was one of those calm evenings, with barely a breeze, filled with the scent of the autumn.

The barn door was open and the glow from the lights inside shone out into the evening. Delphie stood for a moment taking it all in, feeling the anticipation building.

Her long lilac dress felt wonderful, light as air, an ethereal creation of layered chiffon scattered with sparkling sequins around the bodice. The full skirt skimmed her ankles, the perfect length for dancing the quickstep.

Music filtered out from the barn as Kian, Catriona, Callum and others took charge of organising the party as they had done in past years. The band had arrived and set up their chairs and instruments on the small stage, ready to entertain everyone during the evening.

Wil's car was one of the first to arrive, and Delphie's heart squeezed when she saw the tall figure dressed in his classic suit, white shirt and tie, stride towards her, looking the most handsome she'd ever seen him.

His reaction when he saw Delphie assured her that she'd worn the right dress.

'You look beautiful,' Wil said, taking in how lovely she was.

'Shall we go in?' Delphie said, hardly able to contain her excitement.

Wil nodded, and she linked her arm through his to walk into the barn together.

An unexpected cheer arose from those already there.

Callum seemed to be their spokesman as he announced. 'Everyone is grateful for the two of you holding the town's autumn celebration party.'

Another cheer erupted, including from guests walking into the barn, having just arrived.

Everyone was well–dressed and the dance theme had been popular, with guests wearing various styles from tango dresses to ball gowns. Accessories ranged from sparkling tiaras to long strings of beads to go with the twenties era flapper dresses. The men wore suits, from classic evening suits to tuxedos. The three band members wore traditional kilts, ghillie shirts and sporrans.

'My grandparents wished they could be here tonight,' Delphie said to Wil. 'So I've set up my laptop at the side of the bar.'

Wil looked over, and there were her grandparents cheery faces peering out from the screen, enjoying a view of the party. They waved when they saw Delphie and Wil.

The guests began to gather around the edges of the dance floor, clearing it in anticipation of Delphie and Wil's first dance.

'I'll introduce you to my grandparents later,' Delphie promised Wil. But now, it was time for their quickstep.

Delphie nodded to Kian, giving him the cue to start the music as she stood at a corner of the dance floor in hold with Wil.

As the beat kicked in, they were off, dancing across the diagonal, taking their audience by surprise with their speed and stylish moves.

Callum and a couple of other guests filmed the performance with their phones.

Despite the butterflies of excitement, Delphie felt she'd danced the quickstep better than in their rehearsals. The party atmosphere brought out an extra energy in her performance.

Wil raised the bar too, the professional dancer in him evident in his technique and presentation.

As they finished with a flourish, the cheers and applause assured them they'd chosen the right dance to get the night off to an exciting start.

Others took to the dance floor, and Delphie quickly led Wil over to the laptop to meet her grandparents.

'This is my grandmother, Delphine, and my grandfather, Billy.'

'We've heard so much about you, Wil,' her grandmother said to him. 'And what a wonderful quickstep to start the evening.'

'I'm pleased to meet you,' Wil said to them. 'Delphie's told me so much about you too.'

'You look lovely in that dress,' her grandmother said to Delphie.

'I'm changing into another one of your dresses for the closing dance,' Delphie revealed. 'Your pink dress. The one from The Sweetest Waltz painting.'

'Oh, that's great,' her grandmother said, bursting with enthusiasm. 'And we're so pleased to see the two of you. It feels like we're there at the party.'

Her grandfather nudged his wife. 'Tell them,' he urged her. 'I don't think they realise.'

Delphie frowned, wondering what they were talking about. 'Realise what?'

'Your names are the same as ours,' her grandmother explained. 'You're Delphine, named after me. And Billy is William. We presume that you're William too,' she said to Wil.

'Yes,' Wil confirmed.

The penny dropped as Delphie realised the connection of the past and the present.

'It's like history repeating itself,' Billy said to them.

'Maybe you'll find the same type of love and happiness that we've had all these years we've been together,' her grandmother said to Delphie and Wil.

A wave of emotion hit Delphie. Her grandparents were a happy and loving couple. She'd always hoped to have a relationship like that.

Chatting to her grandparents for a few more minutes, Delphie and Wil then waved and headed over to the buffet to meet everyone, and then joined in the dancing.

Delphie danced with others, including Callum and Kian, while Wil whirled Catriona and other ladies around the floor.

'Wil's such a great dancer,' Catriona whispered to Delphie. 'The two of you look like a fine couple.'

This time, Delphie smiled at Catriona, and didn't correct her.

Halfway through the evening the live band had everyone kicking up their heels as they played lively Scottish tunes.

Then the recorded music started again, and Wil danced with Delphie late into the night, pausing sometimes to enjoy the buffet and chat to the guests.

'I'd better hurry over to the farmhouse and change my dress,' Delphie whispered to Wil as the evening was due to end.

'I'll dim the lighting and make sure the music's set up,' said Wil.

Running over to the farmhouse, the night air wafted through the sheer fabric of her lilac dress. And she felt so happy and excited.

After a lightning fast change, she gathered up the long hemline of the pink dress, and ran back over to the barn.

The twinkle lights sparkled like stars around the dance floor that was now illuminated with the spotlights. Wil was standing there waiting for her, having announced to the guests that this was the closing dance of the evening.

The smiling faces encouraged Delphie to take to the dance floor with Wil. Once again, she could see that her grandparents were watching, and Callum and Kian were filming everything.

Wil smiled at her as the music began, and they started to waltz around.

Her pink dress felt light as air and added to the romance of their performance. The guests watched, enjoying them dancing together to the romantic ballad.

The music played, and the song lyrics highlighted their story...

I fell in love with you
When we met by chance
The first time I saw you
It felt like real romance
Through the years we'll be together
In love for ever
One thing will be true
I'll dance the sweetest waltzes with you...

Everyone then joined in for the last dance, waltzing under the lights, having had a wonderful night.

Seeing everyone off as the cars drove away, Delphie and Wil stood together under the vast starry sky arching above them.

Clasping her hand, he gently pulled her close and gazed down at her with all the love in his heart.

'I hope you'll decide to stay here instead of going back to the city,' he said.

Delphie smiled at him. 'Yes, I'm staying.'

She felt his gentle strength pull her even closer to him. 'I have to tell you, that I'm falling deeply in love with you.'

'I feel the same about you, Wil.'

This time when he looked like he was going to kiss her, he didn't pause, and she didn't resist.

The fire and romance ignited between them.

Two shooting stars suddenly soared across the night sky.

'I don't really believe in fairytale signs,' said Delphie, glancing up at the stars.

Wil nodded, though he didn't agree.

'That was a sign, wasn't it?' she said.

'I think so. And if we believe we can do this, be happy together here in the town, we will.'

'Since I came to stay in the farmhouse, I've started to believe in lots of things that I'd long given up on. Like dancing...'

Wil pulled her closer, wrapping her safe in his arms. 'And romance?'

Delphie nodded, and then he kissed her again and again under the star sprinkled night sky.

End

About the Author:

De-ann Black is a bestselling author, scriptwriter and former newspaper journalist. She has over 100 books published. Romance, thrillers, espionage novels, action adventure. And children's books (non-fiction rocket science books and children's fiction). She became an Amazon All-Star author in 2014 and 2015.

She previously worked as a full-time newspaper journalist for several years. She had her own weekly columns in the press. This included being a motoring correspondent where she got to test drive cars every week for the press for three years.

Before being asked to work for the press, De-ann worked in magazine editorial writing everything from fashion features to social news. She was the marketing editor of a glossy magazine.

She is also a professional artist and illustrator. Embroidery design, fabric design, dressmaking, sewing, knitting and fashion are part of her work.

Additionally, De-ann has always been interested in fitness, and was a fitness and bodybuilding champion, 100 metre runner and mountaineer. As a former N.A.B.B.A. Miss Scotland, she had a weekly fitness show on the radio that ran for over three years.

De-ann trained in Shukokai karate, boxing, kickboxing, Dayan Qigong and Jiu Jitsu. She is currently based in Scotland.

Her 16 colouring books are available in paperback, including her latest Summer Nature Colouring Book and Flower Nature Colouring Book.

Her latest embroidery pattern books include: Floral Garden Embroidery Patterns, Christmas & Winter Embroidery Patterns, Floral Spring Embroidery Patterns and Sea Theme Embroidery Patterns.

Website: Find out more at: www.de-annblack.com

Fabric, Wallpaper & Home Decor Collections:
De-ann's fabric designs and wallpaper collections, and home decor items, including her popular Scottish Garden Thistles patterns, are available from Spoonflower.
www.de-annblack.com/spoonflower

Also by De-ann Black (Romance, Action/Thrillers & Children's books). See her Amazon Author page or website for further details about her books, screenplays, illustrations, art, fabric designs and embroidery patterns.

Amazon Author page:
www.De-annBlack.com/Amazon

Romance books:

Music, Dance & Romance series:
1. The Sweetest Waltz

Snow Bells Haven series:
1. Snow Bells Christmas
2. Snow Bells Wedding
3. Love & Lyrics

Scottish Highlands & Island Romance series:
1. Scottish Island Knitting Bee
2. Scottish Island Fairytale Castle
3. Vintage Dress Shop on the Island
4. Fairytale Christmas on the Island

Scottish Loch Romance series:
1. Sewing & Mending Cottage
2. Scottish Loch Summer Romance
3. Sweet Music

Quilting Bee & Tea Shop series:
1. The Quilting Bee
2. The Tea Shop by the Sea
3. Embroidery Cottage
4. Knitting Shop by the Sea
5. Christmas Weddings

The Cure for Love Romance series:
1. The Cure for Love
2. The Cure for Love at Christmas

Sewing, Crafts & Quilting series:
1. The Sewing Bee
2. The Sewing Shop
3. Knitting Cottage (Scottish Highland romance)
4. Scottish Highlands Christmas Wedding

Cottages, Cakes & Crafts series:
1. The Flower Hunter's Cottage
2. The Sewing Bee by the Sea
3. The Beemaster's Cottage
4. The Chocolatier's Cottage
5. The Bookshop by the Seaside
6. The Dressmaker's Cottage

Scottish Chateau, Colouring & Crafts series:
1. Christmas Cake Chateau
2. Colouring Book Cottage

Summer Sewing Bee

Sewing, Knitting & Baking series:
1. The Tea Shop
2. The Sewing Bee & Afternoon Tea
3. The Christmas Knitting Bee
4. Champagne Chic Lemonade Money
5. The Vintage Sewing & Knitting Bee

Tea Dress Shop series:
1. The Tea Dress Shop At Christmas
2. The Fairytale Tea Dress Shop In Edinburgh
3. The Vintage Tea Dress Shop In Summer

The Tea Shop & Tearoom series:
1. The Christmas Tea Shop & Bakery
2. The Christmas Chocolatier
3. The Chocolate Cake Shop in New York at Christmas
4. The Bakery by the Seaside
5. Shed in the City

Christmas Romance series:
1. Christmas Romance in Paris
2. Christmas Romance in Scotland

Oops! I'm the Paparazzi series:
1. Oops! I'm the Paparazzi
2. Oops! I'm Up To Mischief
3. Oops! I'm the Paparazzi, Again

The Bitch-Proof Suit series:
1. The Bitch-Proof Suit
2. The Bitch-Proof Romance
3. The Bitch-Proof Bride
4. The Bitch-Proof Wedding

Heather Park: Regency Romance
Dublin Girl
Why Are All The Good Guys Total Monsters?
I'm Holding Out For A Vampire Boyfriend

Action/Thriller books:
Knight in Miami
Agency Agenda
Love Him Forever
Someone Worse
Electric Shadows
The Strife Of Riley
Shadows Of Murder
Cast a Dark Shadow

Children's books:
Faeriefied
Secondhand Spooks
Poison-Wynd
Wormhole Wynd
Science Fashion
School For Aliens

Colouring books:
Summer Nature
Flower Nature
Summer Garden
Spring Garden
Autumn Garden
Sea Dream
Festive Christmas
Christmas Garden
Christmas Theme
Flower Bee
Wild Garden
Faerie Garden Spring
Flower Hunter
Stargazer Space
Bee Garden
Scottish Garden
Seasons

Embroidery Design books:
Sea Theme Embroidery Patterns
Floral Garden Embroidery Patterns
Christmas & Winter Embroidery Patterns
Floral Spring Embroidery Patterns
Floral Nature Embroidery Designs
Scottish Garden Embroidery Designs

Printed in Great Britain
by Amazon